Running Stitches

a quilting cozy

Carol Dean Jones

Text copyright © 2018
by Carol Dean Jones

Photography and artwork copyright
© 2018 by C&T Publishing, Inc.

Publisher: Amy Marson

Creative Director: Gailen Runge

Acquisitions Editor: Roxane Cerda

Managing Editor: Liz Aneloski

Project Writer: Teresa Stroin

Technical Editor / Illustrator:
Linda Johnson

Cover/Book Designer: April Mostek

Production Coordinator:
Tim Manibusan

Production Editor: Alice Mace Nakanishi

Photo Assistant: Mai Yong Vang

Cover photography by Lucy Glover and
Mai Yong Vang of C&T Publishing, Inc.

Cover quilt: *Time Passes*, 2003,
by the author

Library of Congress Cataloging-in-
Publication Data

Names: Jones, Carol Dean, author.

Title: Running stitches : a quilting cozy /
Carol Dean Jones.

Description: Lafayette, CA :
C&T Publishing, Inc., [2018] | Series:
A quilting cozy series ; book 2

Identifiers: LCCN 2018003518 |
ISBN 9781617457500

Subjects: LCSH: Quilting--Fiction. |
Missing persons--Investigation--Fiction. |
GSAFD: Mystery fiction.

Classification: LCC PS3610.O6224 R86
2018 | DDC 813/.6--dc23

LC record available at
https://lccn.loc.gov/2018003518

Printed in the USA

10 9 8 7 6 5 4 3 2 1

A Quilting Cozy Series

by Carol Dean Jones

Left Holding the Bag (book 10)

Tattered & Torn (book 9)

Missing Memories (book 8)

The Rescue Quilt (book 7)

Moon Over the Mountain (book 6)

Stitched Together (book 5)

Patchwork Connections (book 4)

Sea Bound (book 3)

Running Stitches (book 2)

Tie Died (book 1)

*Dedicated with love to
Barbara, Forester, and
Gweneth*

Acknowledgments

My sincere appreciation goes to my friends, Phyllis Inscoe and Janice Packard, as well as to my sister, Pamela Kimmell, for all their encouragement, critiques, and suggestions along the way.

Prologue

There was no trial. Andy agreed to a plea bargain and was sentenced to five years in the local minimum-security prison farm. It was clear to everyone that Andy was no criminal. He killed his brother in the equivalent of a bar fight, which took place in Andy's living room. George had burst in, belligerent and angry, and they'd fought as they had since they were young boys.

It was an accident, and Andy probably wouldn't have been charged if he hadn't left town. But he returned home and was arrested. Andy was sorry about killing his brother, but he was mostly sorry that they'd never resolved their differences. He missed his brother, or maybe he just missed the idea of a brother. Andy was a kind and caring man.

No one expected that Andy would escape, but that's exactly what he did.

Chapter 1

"It's spectacular!" Sarah exclaimed as Ruth and her daughter Katie hung the quilt behind the cash register. "I've never seen a quilt like that! What's it called?" Sarah was a new quilter and had limited exposure to the world of quilts.

"This is called a sampler. We used fabrics from the Civil War–reproduction collection and these are all blocks that were popular during the mid-1800s," Ruth explained.

Katie spoke up saying, "It's possible that some of these blocks were used by the Underground Railroad as secret codes to communicate with runaway slaves."

"Fascinating!" Sarah said. "I'd love to know more about that."

"We'll be talking about all this in our next class," Ruth responded. "In fact," she added as she stood back and admired the quilt, "this would be a good quilt for you to make, Sarah, since you would learn all these different techniques."

"I love it," Sarah exclaimed.

Ruth Weaver owned Running Stitches, or as her customers fondly called it, Stitches. Ruth and Katie, her twenty-year-old daughter, provided a wide range of high-end quilting fabrics, all the necessary tools and implements, and an endless supply of books and patterns. The walls of the shop were covered with quilts made primarily by Katie who, along with her mother, taught classes for both the advanced quilter and those with nothing more than a desire to learn.

Sarah had been in that last category. After her husband died, she had saved his ties, hoping to use them to make a quilt for her daughter, Martha. Unfortunately, Sarah had no idea where to start and came to Stitches as a novice. Ruth and Katie had patiently guided her through the fundamentals and, as a result, Sarah had become quite proficient.

"Wouldn't this be too advanced for me?" Sarah asked.

"No. I'm calling this an advanced class, but I'll be teaching the simplest blocks first and, by the time we get to the more difficult blocks, you'll be ready."

Sarah examined the quilt more closely. "I bought many of these fabrics for the quilt I was planning for Charles."

"Have you used those fabrics yet?" Ruth asked.

"No," Sarah responded, thinking about the quilt she was planning to make for her friend, Charles. "Maybe I'll sign up for this class and make this one for him instead. It's historical, and I think he would like that."

Sarah and Charles had met many years before she moved to Cunningham Village; he was the policeman who came to her door almost twenty years ago to inform her of the accident that had taken the life of her husband, Jonathan. Despite the anguish of that day, the kindness of this gentle man stood out. After she moved to the Village, they met again. He was retired, as was she, and both were starting a new chapter of their lives.

"He's smitten," her feisty friend, Sophie, had said the day she met him. Sarah was not at all ready for *smitten* and tried hard not to give Charles any encouragement. But she liked him and he'd become a very special friend.

Sarah had moved to Cunningham Village the previous year at the insistence of her daughter, Martha, and against her own better judgment. But as it turned out, Martha was absolutely right.

Cunningham Village was a retirement community with independent villas, a center with all the recreational and educational services a person could want, and a continuing care component, which was available to seniors who needed more care.

That was Sarah's original objection—the concept of a retirement village made her feel old. Or maybe, in her late sixties, it was just a reminder that *old* was a state rapidly approaching. But once she made the move, got to know her neighbors, and got involved in the activities, she quickly adjusted to her new life. Quilting had become an essential part of that new life.

After signing up for the class and buying a few more fabrics from Ruth's Civil War collection, Sarah drove home, again turning her thoughts to Charles. They were clearly becoming close, but she wasn't sure just where she wanted it to go. But, wherever it was headed, she knew she wanted it to go there slowly.

Jonathan had been her first and only love and, for some reason she couldn't explain, her growing relationship with Charles was causing her to feel disloyal to Jon's memory. She felt that Charles would understand. He had lost his wife many years ago and still looked wistful when he talked about her.

All of Sarah's concerns vanished when she opened her front door and was met by the enthusiasm and love of her precious dog, Barney. Barney ran in circles and snuggled in close to her with every muscle trembling in an attempt to keep from jumping up on her. "Good boy, Barney!" She told him, appreciating his effort. "Let's go for a walk." Barney ran to the hook and tugged on his leash, dragging it to her and dropping it at her feet. "Good boy," she repeated, clapping her hands. Barney smiled.

Sarah adopted Barney from the local Humane Society the previous year. There had been a murder on her block, and she originally wanted him for protection, but they'd become fast friends. He was a medium-size dog of no particular, recognizable breed. He had big brown eyes, almost the color of his coat. He was ever so slightly cross-eyed. He had a long snout of a nose and rather longish whiskers that twitched when he opened his mouth. When Sarah first saw him, she thought he was undoubtedly the homeliest dog she had ever seen, but he was most certainly smiling at her. Sarah had looked at his short wagging tail, his straggly coat, and she smiled back. He looked at her with appreciation. They'd made an instant connection. She had to have him. He had to have her.

Together they went out into the brisk night air and strolled up the block. The homes on her block, as well as on most of the blocks in the Village, were one-story villas attached in groups of five. As she passed Andy's empty house, she thought about the tragedy that occurred there the previous year, resulting in Andy being sentenced to a few years in prison. She was eager for the day he'd be back home. She missed her friend.

"What're you and that ugly dog doing out there in the middle of the night?" Sophie hollered from her door. She already had her pink elephant pajamas on and had her trench coat over her shoulders as she walked toward them.

"I could ask the same question of you. You look like you're ready for bed," Sarah responded, "… and Barney's not ugly!" she added.

Sophie walked hurriedly toward Sarah and Barney. Sophie was a short rotund woman in her mid-seventies. She had an infectious laugh that could be heard up and down the block as she told her greatly embellished versions of the many happenings around the Village.

Sophie was also one of the kindest people Sarah had ever met. She took newcomers under her wing and helped them with what could be a particularly traumatic experience as they moved into a retirement community. She had been Sarah's first friend and they'd remained close. Right now, however, Sophie looked worried.

"I need to tell you something, and it's not good news, Sarah."

Sarah stopped walking and turned to meet Sophie. Barney stretched out on the sidewalk and rested his head on his front paws. "What is it, Sophie?" Sarah asked with apprehension.

"That young policewoman called me today and asked if we've had any contact with Andy."

"We talk to him every few weeks! Did you tell her that?" Sarah asked frowning. "Why does she want to know anyway?"

"I told her about our phone calls to the prison. That wasn't what she wanted to know. She wanted to know if he has been around here."

"Around here?" Sarah responded looking bewildered. "How could he have been around here? He's in prison."

"That's just it," Sophie said as she glanced down to hide the tears that were beginning to collect in her eyes. "He escaped, Sarah."

"*What?*" Sarah cried out. "How could he do that?" Andy was scheduled to be released in a couple of years and, with good behavior, maybe sooner. "He's ruined it for himself again! What's wrong with that man?" Sarah was clearly upset and disappointed with Andy. She and Sophie had stood by him through his trial and tried to make prison life easier for him by writing and phoning often. "He hasn't said a word that would suggest this was on his mind," she added with a deep frown. "Why would he do it?"

"How well do we really know Andy?" Sophie asked rhetorically. "He's been a great friend and neighbor, but there's much about Andy we don't know." It was during the investigation that Sophie and Sarah had first learned about Andy's history with alcohol. Then he ran off to Florida rather than admit to the fight he had with his brother that resulted in his brother's death. "And don't forget," Sophie added, "he let us think he was dead for several months! That was not kind!" Sophie was obviously disappointed with Andy.

Sarah shook her head and sighed. "Let's get some sleep, Sophie. We'll talk tomorrow, and we'll call that policewoman. What was her name, Amanda? Amanda something?"

"Amanda Holmes. She's still working with Detective Gabriel. Maybe we can go by and talk to both of them. This is just crazy!" Sophie said, shaking her head as she turned to leave. "Why would he do this?" she muttered to herself.

Sophie headed toward her house without saying goodbye. Sarah was confused by the news. At first, she felt angry with Andy but then realized there must be some explanation. She hoped she would find out soon. The previous year, she'd spent many weeks worrying about what had happened to Andy. She and Sophie even got involved in the investigation, much to the police department's annoyance. She wasn't eager to start worrying about him again. Sarah slowly headed for her front door. Barney got up, stretched, and lumbered after her.

Sarah turned and watched the house across the street as Sophie's lights went off, one after the other as she made her way toward her bedroom. Sarah sighed and said, "Come on, Barney. Let's get some sleep. I think tomorrow is going to be a long day." Barney sighed and followed her into the house.

Chapter 2

A ndy watched as the busload of prisoners approached. The gate opened, and the guard waved them through. Andy continued to watch as the men got off and lined up along the side of the bus. There were only eight. *A motley looking group*, he thought. But he knew they weren't hardened criminals. Evanston was a minimum security prison. He felt lucky to be there. He knew it could've been much worse.

The men walked single file toward the building and, one by one, disappeared inside. Andy focused on one, a guy with carrot-red hair and a gray beard. He looked familiar, but from this distance Andy couldn't be sure.

Hours later the man approached Andy in the mess hall. A guard followed at a distance but kept an eye on him. *They always watched the new guys*. Some men were sent to Evanston who couldn't handle the freedom. The guards identified them early on and shipped them out.

"Andy? Andy Burgess?" The man said incredulously. "What the heck are you doing here? I heard you quit drinking, cleaned up your act, and moved to some old folks home over in Middletown."

"Yeah, well, some habits die hard," Andy responded not wanting to say too much.

The carrot-topped man was Bryce Silverman. Andy knew Bryce fifteen or so years before during his heavy drinking days. They didn't have much to talk about now.

"Really, man," the guy asked again. "What're you in for?"

"I got in some trouble," Andy responded vaguely.

A tall lanky guy with a pock-marked face was standing nearby. With a cigarette dangling from his dry lips and a wicked smile, he interjected, "Come on, man, you don't know?" He sneered and dropped his cigarette to the floor. "This guy offed his own brother!"

"George?" Carrot-top asked, looking surprised. "You killed George? I thought George was in prison for life!" Then he added with a chuckle, "Short life, I guess."

Andy didn't want to tell his story. He didn't even want to think about it. It was an accident. He knew it. The judge knew it. But all that was in the past. As far as he knew, the guys here didn't know anything about him. But, in fact, rumors spread fast.

"You see any of the old gang?" Andy asked, not actually caring but, at least, it changed the subject.

"Nah. Most of the old bunch has scattered." Then he added with more enthusiasm, "I did see your old girlfriend a couple months ago before she ran off."

"Catherine?" Andy said with surprise. "What do you mean *ran off*?"

"You know she married ol' Buck, right?"

"Yeah," Andy replied, looking down at the food remaining on his plate in order to avoid Carrot-top's eyes. Finally, without looking up, Andy repeated, "So, Bryce, what do you mean *ran off*?"

"She just up and left. Buck was fighting mad, but he didn't seem to care where she went. He just wanted to find the guy."

"What guy?" Andy asked, still not looking at Silverman.

"She'd been hanging out with this guy. No one knew his name or where he came from, but they hung around the bar together when Buck was working the night shift. Sometimes they would leave together. We all suspected the two of them took off, but no one told Buck anything. You know Buck's temper. No one wanted to hassle with him."

"Hmm." Andy added, trying to seem only mildly interested, "What about the kid?"

"Catherine's kid? Hell, I don't know. Last I heard she took off, too."

"With Catherine?"

"No. It was a month or so later. We figured Buck drove her off. He was drinkin' more than usual and fightin' mad all the time. She probably couldn't take it."

"… only fourteen," Andy muttered. "… where would she go?"

"To the streets, I guess," Bryce responded, shrugging his shoulders. "That's where most girls go."

* * * * *

Andy lay in his bunk. It was late. No clocks were around, so he didn't know how late. It had been dark for hours and he laid there trying to keep his mind a blank slate. He didn't want to think, but as his eyelids drooped he became less able to control his thoughts. He could see Catherine clearly to this day, fifteen years later. She would have been a beautiful woman if her life had gone another way. But she had been on the streets too. She ran off from home when she was thirteen and supported herself with what she could get from men. Andy hung out with her for a while, but it never was serious. His wife had died, and he was mourning. Probably still was, for that matter.

He remembered the last time he saw Catherine. "Andy, I don't want to marry you. Thanks for offering. You're a real standup guy, but you're much too old for me. You're older than my dad!" she had said, giving him a playful slap on the arm. Then in a more serious tone, she added, "Buck wants to marry me, and he thinks the baby is his. I didn't tell him any different." She looked away and added, "We're getting married next week."

Andy knew it was his baby. He even knew the night she was conceived. But he didn't argue. If she wanted to marry Buck, so be it. He heard she named the girl Caitlyn.

"Caitlyn," he said her name aloud.

He wondered where she was right now. He would find her. He was her dad, and she needed him.

Andy was trusted by the prison guards. Two guards had even been sitting in on his computer class. Administrative staff joked with Andy and had told him that he would, most likely, be paroled at his next hearing. No one paid attention to him in the yard.

The next morning he simply walked off the grounds while the guards were busy assigning work detail.

Chapter 3

Sarah sat in Ruth's sampler class waiting for the other students. She glanced down the class list and only recognized one name, Dottie Ramsey. Ruth was still working out front, waiting for her daughter, Katie, to arrive and take over the shop. Ruth was, however, in and out of the classroom. She handed out the instruction sheet for the first class which was the Log Cabin block. "Please read the instructions and help yourselves to coffee and cookies," she called back as she was leaving to take care of a customer.

Sarah knew she was going to have trouble concentrating on the class. She was worried about Andy. A week had gone by since she learned that he'd left the prison but still no word from him. She and Sophie had stopped by the police station to see Officer Holmes. Amanda was not in the office, but Detective Gabriel spoke with them.

Detective Gabriel had met with the prison staff, and they were all stunned that Andy had left the grounds. Andy's mood had been upbeat and he had recently volunteered to teach basic computer skills to a group of inmates. He seemed to be enjoying the class and was looking forward to his first parole hearing.

Sarah and Sophie got to know Detective Gabriel the previous year and liked the man. Known as Gabe to his friends, Detective Gabriel had a kindness about him that caused Sarah to wonder how he could do police work, but often his pleasant approach worked to his advantage.

Sarah knew Andy would contact her eventually, but she dreaded seeing him. Her alliances were torn between Andy and the detectives. She liked Amanda and felt they were developing a special friendship. Amanda was a quilter, although she was usually too busy to enjoy it. She occasionally attended the Friday Night Quilters, a group that met weekly at Ruth's shop to share their love for quilting.

Sarah had promised to let Amanda know if Andy were to contact her. On the other hand, Andy was her friend and she owed him her loyalty. She had no idea what she would do when she heard from him. And she was sure she *would* hear from him. She tried to turn her attention back to the class.

The other students had arrived and there were four that Sarah hadn't met. As they drank coffee and talked, she learned their names and a little bit about their quilting experience. Delores was a seasoned quilter but was taking the class with her granddaughter who was excited about learning to quilt. Sarah had seen Delores' work at the county fair where she often won ribbons.

Delores' granddaughter was only fifteen and a freshman in high school. She was spending time with her grandmother while her military parents were temporarily deployed out of the country. Delores felt that the sampler quilt would give her granddaughter a variety of experience with different designs and techniques.

Sarah figured that Delores must be in her late sixties, about her own age. "Do you live in Cunningham Village?" Sarah asked her.

"Yes, as a matter of fact. I just moved there. And you?"

"Me too. Have you been to the community center yet?" Sarah asked.

"No, actually I haven't been anywhere yet. I'm eager to learn my way around." Sarah made a mental note to get Delores and Sophie together. Sophie had been instrumental in getting Sarah integrated into the community. She knew everyone and was eager to help the newbies get acclimated.

"This is my granddaughter, Danielle," Delores added putting her hand on her granddaughter's shoulder to guide her closer to Sarah. "… and this is Sarah Miller. She lives in the Village too."

"Hi, Danielle. I'm glad you came. This should be a good class."

"Thank you, Ms. Miller."

"Just call me Sarah if it's okay with your grandmother. We're very informal here."

"Okay, I will. But please call me Danny. I've never liked being called Danielle."

"I don't see why not," her grandmother huffed. "It's a perfectly good name, and it was sure good enough for my sister." The two got into a good natured squabble. It sounded like it was not the first time this issue had come up. They went back to their seats arm in arm; Sarah knew all was forgiven.

Delores and Danny. Sarah made a mental note of their names; it was getting harder to remember people's names, especially now that she was meeting so many new people.

She kept hearing that it was perfectly normal to be forgetful, but after a certain age one couldn't help but worry. She had seen the forlorn folks in the nursing home suffering from various forms of dementia and was determined never to join them.

The other two students were sisters, Christina and Kimberly. The two women were in their late forties and had never married. They explained that they lived on the edge of town in a Sears Roebuck Catalog Home which had been left to them by their family. Sarah was fascinated by the homes and asked when it was built. Christina said their grandfather had ordered their ready-to-assemble home as a kit from the Sears Roebuck catalog in the mid-1930s. Her grandfather had told her it was delivered by boxcar, and he and his brothers had assembled it!

"That's incredible!" Sarah said. "And it's still standing!"

"Not only standing, but improved!" Kimberly added proudly. "Granddad was able to buy the add-on kits in the 1940s: electricity, plumbing, central heating. My father did a lot of improvements too. My parents lived there with grandmother until she died in 1991. Granny couldn't do the steps, so Dad added a bedroom and bath on the first floor for her. Our parents both died a couple of years ago, and Christina and I moved in. It's a terrific little house with lots of history."

"That's just fascinating," Sarah said. "I'd love to see it sometime."

"Maybe we can get together to do some sewing on our sampler once we know what we're doing. We'd love to have you come over," Christina offered.

"Sounds like fun!" Sarah responded. *Christina and Kimberly*. Sarah added their names to her memory list.

About that time, Dottie joined the group. Sarah knew Dottie from previous classes and, as always, Dottie entered the room like a tornado with fabric dangling out of her tote bag and red curls escaping from her scrunchies. "Oh, those kids!" She said as she plopped down at the table, dropping her tote on the floor. Two spools of thread rolled under the table. "They'll be the death of me yet," she added.

Dottie had two boys and a girl but, most likely, the problem was not the children but, rather, Dottie's haphazard life style. She was always rushed, always late, always seeming to be in a dither about something.

"Were we supposed to bring something tonight?" Dottie asked, looking at Sarah's fabrics.

By the time Ruth returned to the classroom, Dottie's tote bag had fallen over, and most of its contents were strewn across the floor. She attempted to pull them closer to her chair so Ruth could get by.

It turned out to be a successful class. Sarah felt totally confident making her first block for the sampler. In the spring, Sarah had made a throw using Log Cabin blocks, so she was comfortable with the technique.

Sarah had decided to buy ten more fat quarters in the Civil War–reproduction line but in light colors, primarily tan and cream with small prints in pale blue, brown, or green. She used the light ones for the logs on one side of the block and an assortment of dark fabrics for the opposite sides.

Sarah had planned to follow tradition and put red in the center to represent the fire burning in the center of the *cabin*, but she noticed that the Log Cabin block in Ruth's sampler had a black center. "Why is the center of this block black instead of red?" Sarah asked.

"I was just getting ready to talk about that, Sarah." While the women worked, Ruth told the story of the Underground Railroad quilts.

"Now, some people don't believe these stories," Ruth began. "There's no written proof, but there have been many stories passed down through families about quilts being used to help slaves escape. Since the slaves weren't permitted to learn to read, quilts may have contained coded messages about safe escape routes. For example, the block we're doing today, the Log Cabin but with a black center instead of red, is said to have been hung outside of a house that was a safe house, a *station* along the escape route that would offer a safe place to rest or get food and clothing. Other patterns may have pointed out the safest route to Ohio or Canada which were the destinations for most of the runaway slaves."

The class was mesmerized by the stories as Ruth talked. Most of the class, except Dottie, had stopped working to listen while looking at the sample quilt that Ruth had moved into the classroom. Dottie was still going through her fabrics, looking for ones she wanted to use for the quilt.

Kimberly raised her hand timidly, and Ruth immediately acknowledged her. "I think I've seen the center of the Log Cabin block done with yellow. Does that have any particular significance?"

"Not in the stories about the Underground Railroad quilt, but in traditional Log Cabin quilts the center is sometimes yellow to represent a friendly light in the window."

Kimberly nodded her acknowledgement with a smile.

"The Bear Paw pattern," Ruth continued, pointing to the paw block, "may have told the runaway to follow the trail left by the bears as they crossed the mountains. We'll be doing that block in a couple of weeks."

"And these Underground Railroad stories may not even be true?" Sarah asked.

"We just don't know, but there are so many stories passed down through the families of both the abolitionists and the freed slaves that we can only assume there's some truth to them." Ruth continued to tell brief stories about the other blocks and added, "We'll talk more about these as we make them." She then went over the instructions and demonstrated the first few steps.

Later Ruth walked around the room, looking at the blocks her students were working on. Some were beginning to sew their strips together, and others were still cutting. "Don't forget the importance of a consistent quarter-inch seam," she said. "That's how you'll ensure that your blocks come out the right size."

The class ran late, and it was dark when Sarah packed up her supplies. She was the last person to leave, following Ruth out as she locked up. "Do you need a ride?" Ruth asked, looking around and not seeing Sarah's car.

"No, I'm parked on the side of the shop," Sarah responded. As she turned the corner and approached her car, she was aware of the darkness in the alley. *I'm going to park on the street from now on*, she told herself. Ruth had mentioned moving the class to mornings. Fumbling in the darkness, Sarah hoped that's what Ruth would do. Sarah turned on the miniature flashlight attached to her key chain and guided the key into the lock.

"Pssst."

What was that? She hurried to open the car door.

"Sarah! Over here."

Sarah pointed her flashlight in the direction of the voice, but the light was too weak to shed light on the speaker. "Who are you," she demanded in as confident a tone as she could manage. She tried to hold the flashlight steady.

"It's Andy," the voice announced. "Let me get into the back seat, okay?"

Sarah hesitated, but she was so eager to talk with him that she was willing to take the chance. In her mind, she could hear Detective Shields' accusations of *aiding and abetting*, but she had to remind herself that Shields was long gone and unable to threaten her with prosecution as he did the previous year. "Get in," she whispered, "and stay down." *What am I doing?*

Chapter 4

"Get dressed fast. I'm picking you up in a few minutes," Sarah announced as Sophie answered the phone.

"Sarah, have you lost your mind? It's nearly 10:00, and I'm in my pajamas. Why do you want to pick me up?" Sophie asked with annoyance.

"Just be ready and get into the car quickly without saying a word no matter what you see, okay? We don't know who might be watching."

"Is it Andy?" Sophie asked.

"Be ready!" Sarah retorted and clicked the cell phone off.

A few minutes later Sarah pulled into Sophie's driveway and stopped behind Sophie's black Jeep. As Sophie locked her door and approached the car, Sarah could see her muttering to herself. Her clothes were askew, and her pink elephant pajamas were protruding from her pant legs. As she walked in front of the car and opened the passenger's door, she glanced into the back seat. Her eyebrows shot up her forehead, and her eyes opened wide. "Not a word, Sophie," Sarah demanded. "Get in and face front. Don't look back."

Then she added, "Andy, stay on the floor and don't talk."

"But ..." Sophie began to object.

"Okay," came a small voice from the floor of the back seat.

"Sophie, get in!" Sarah ordered impatiently. Sophie huffed but got in. Sarah backed out of the driveway and headed for the main gate. "Andy, stay down low. We're passing the security gate." Andy balled himself up tighter on the floor. As they drove past the gate and headed up the street, he rose up onto the seat but continued to stoop down low.

"What's going on?" Sophie asked, still staring forward as instructed.

"Andy wants to talk to the two of us, and it isn't safe for him to come into the community. The security guards have certainly been warned to watch for him."

Still staring straight ahead, Sophie quietly said, "Hi, Andy."

"Hi, Sophie," a timid voice came from the backseat. "I'm sorry," the voice added meekly.

"We know," Sarah said tenderly. "We know." Turning to Sophie, Sarah said, "I'm thinking we could go down by the river. We can park along the road near the hobo camp. I think we'll be safe there."

"Why don't we park and go into the camp," Sophie suggested. "The guys will be there and can act as lookout for us. I know they'll want to see Andy. What do you think, Andy?" Sophie asked without looking back.

"I think we should stay to ourselves. The less people who know about me the better," Andy responded. "Let's just park and talk in the car." They found a secluded spot where they could pull off the main road.

Sophie and Sarah turned in their seats so they could see Andy. "Okay, Andy," Sophie demanded, "What in Sam Hill is going on with you?" She sounded angry but, in fact, she was simply worried about him. He'd been a close friend for many years, but he seemed to be digging a hole for himself which was getting deeper and deeper. "Why did you leave the prison?"

* * * * *

Sarah and Sophie got home after midnight and, without discussing it, both went into Sarah's house. Sarah let Barney out in the backyard, and Sophie put the tea kettle on. "What do you have to eat?" Sophie asked as Sarah came back in.

"I have the remains of Charles' birthday cake," Sarah responded as she headed for the fridge." The two women were unusually quiet, each processing what she had learned from Andy in her own way.

Finally, Sophie spoke up. "I think Andy's plan is doomed to failure."

Sarah shrugged. "Well, I don't see how he can be on the streets looking for Caitlyn without getting caught. And if he's caught, he'll be in prison for many years!"

"Besides that," Sophie responded, "he doesn't even know what she looks like! How can he possibly find her?"

Earlier that night, parked by the river, Andy had done most of the talking. He told Sarah and Sophie about his ex-girlfriend and the fact that she had run off, leaving her husband, Buck, and her fourteen-year-old daughter.

He told them that the daughter, Caitlyn, was, in fact, his daughter. Tears ran down his cheeks as he talked. "I left Hamilton after Catherine's wedding before the baby was born. I've tried to forget about the little girl, but I haven't been able to. Whenever I see a kid, I wonder how she is and what she looks like."

"You never saw her?" Sarah had asked.

"No, not really," Andy responded. "I went by the school once when she was about eight. I watched the kids in the playground, and I spotted a little girl that looked just like Catherine. Maybe it was her." The tears flowed down his cheeks. "Maybe it wasn't. I'm her dad, and I don't even know what she looks like."

He still hadn't said exactly why he left the prison, but they were getting the idea. "So, Andy. Did you leave the prison to try to find her?" Sophie asked.

"That's it," he responded. "I'm no kind of a dad, but she doesn't have anybody. And it's dangerous out there."

"Out where?" Sophie asked, sounding confused.

"Well, on the street, I guess. I'm just assuming she's up in Hamilton; that's where Catherine and Buck were living. And, unless she has friends that'll take her in, I'm afraid she's just living on the street. Maybe not, but I have to find out. I have to make sure she's safe."

The city of Hamilton was only about thirty-five miles from Middletown. When Jonathan was alive, he and Sarah went from Middletown to Hamilton often, but since he died, and especially since moving to Cunningham Village, Sarah rarely went there. There had been nice shops in the downtown area but, with shopping malls so convenient in Middletown, there was no reason to make the trip.

Hamilton had a decidedly ritzy side with big Victorian homes, but it also had the part of town that Sarah's generation referred to as the *other side of the tracks*. In recent years, it wasn't safe to go into the east side because of crime and drugs. Sarah was glad Middletown had remained a quiet little town. The thought of a fourteen-year-old girl trying to make her way in Hamilton was frightening.

"How can we help?" Sarah had asked, gently reaching back to pat Andy's hand.

"I don't want to involve you ladies," Andy had responded. "I just wanted you to know the whole story. Please don't be mad at me. I need to make sure my daughter is okay. She doesn't have anyone right now."

Sarah and Sophie continued to sit at Sarah's table thinking about their conversation with Andy. The chocolate cake sat untouched. Finally, Sarah spoke up.

"Maybe we should check Andy's tie quilt and see if there is anything hidden in it. If there's any money, that would help Andy right now. I'm sure he can't get to his bank account since the police will be watching for him."

"I have a better idea," Sophie offered. "Let's get some sleep and talk about this in the morning. Things always look clearer after a good night's sleep and a fresh pot of coffee … and chocolate cake," she added.

"I agree. Come over when you get up and we'll figure out just how involved we should get in this mess."

Sarah was exhausted and looked forward to crawling into her bed. "I need a quilt for my bed," she realized. "That will be my next project." Barney put his paws up on her bed and nuzzled her neck. She scratched his ears and said, "Good night, sweet dog. Get in your bed." Barney sighed and got into his foam sided bed, scratched at the covers, made three clockwise turns, and curled up nose to tail. Sarah heard another deep sigh, and Barney was gone for the night.

Sarah was not so lucky. Although she was extremely tired and had expected she would fall right to sleep, her mind wandered to Andy's quilt. It was still in the wardrobe where she had stored it for him the previous year. She wondered whether there was anything of value inside it. Andy's brother got himself killed over the possibility that something had been hidden in the quilt—something that could lead to a possible fortune. *Sophie and I'll take a look tomorrow,* she decided as she finally drifted off to sleep.

Chapter 5

A nother week had passed and no further word was received from Andy. Sarah and Sophie were getting worried about what might have happened to him. Sarah called Amanda at the police station to see if perhaps he'd been recaptured. "Good Morning, Officer Holmes," she began.

"Hello Sarah. I was hoping you would call. Have you seen Andy?"

Sarah didn't want to lie to Amanda, but she didn't want to betray Andy's trust. She managed to avoid answering by responding, "That's just what I wanted to ask you. I'm worried about him."

"Well, there's been no word from Andy on this end, but then I hardly expect him to just walk into the station. I wish he hadn't done this to himself. He might have gotten released at his next parole hearing. Gabe talked to the prison folks and learned he had been a model prisoner. His computer class was going along, and everyone liked him."

Sarah was relieved that she didn't have to answer Amanda's question. An idea was taking form in her mind.

"Tell me, Amanda, what would happen if he did turn himself in? Would that work in his favor?"

"Why do you ask?" Amanda responded, with a note of suspicion in her voice.

Oh my. I've said too much. "I was just wondering since you said it was unlikely that he would turn himself in. I just wondered what would happen if he did."

Amanda suspected Sarah knew more than she was sharing but decided to play it out. "It would work in his favor, for sure."

"In what way?" Sarah asked.

"Well, the judge would take it into consideration when deciding what the penalty would be for escaping. He would also consider the reason Andy took off."

"What do you mean?" Sarah asked.

She knows something, Amanda thought. "Well, he may have had a very good reason—sickness in the family, something like that. The judge would take that into consideration, as well. It would definitely work to his advantage if he were simply to turn himself in."

Sarah remained quiet as a plan began to materialize in her mind. She would need to talk to Charles about it. "Thank you, Amanda. I appreciate you talking to me about it. We're all worried about Andy."

"It was good talking with you, Sarah. Remember, you need to call us if you learn anything. I wouldn't want you to be caught up in this by helping him. You know you would be guilty of harboring a fugitive, and there would be repercussions." Amanda admired Sarah and felt terrible about threatening her, but it was for Sarah's own good to be reminded that helping Andy was a crime.

The minute she hung up, Sarah picked the phone up and called Charles. "We need to talk," she said as he answered the phone.

"This sounds ominous," he responded with a chuckle.

"It's serious, Charles. It's about Andy."

"I'll be right there."

She then dialed Sophie. "Can you come over? Charles is on his way. We three need to talk."

"You told Charles?" Sophie bellowed. "What did I tell you about that? He's a retired cop, and his alliances are with the department. He'll turn Andy in. He'll have to!" Sophie was extremely upset, and her voice was shaking despite the volume.

"Sophie, I have a plan, and we need Charles. Come on over. I think we can help Andy best this way."

The three friends settled around Sarah's kitchen table. Sarah placed the coffee pot on a trivet in the middle of the table along with a coffee cake she had quickly made from a mix. Sophie poured coffee for everyone and sighed. "Okay, Toots. What's this all about?"

"What would the two of you think about playing detective?" Sarah responded.

"What do you have in mind," Charles asked suspiciously.

"This is what I'm thinking," Sarah explained. "Let's see if we can convince Andy to voluntarily turn himself in to Amanda. She has led me to believe that he could minimize the sentence the court would impose if he turned himself in and if he had a good reason for running off in the first place."

"And what might that reason be?" Charles asked. "And what do you know about all this? Have you seen Andy?" His voice was accusatory.

"Please don't use that tone with me, Charles," Sarah said. "I'm not a criminal."

"You are if you're harboring a fugitive," he responded with a frown.

"Told you so!" Sophie said to Sarah, holding herself in her famous peacock position. "I knew you shouldn't involve him."

"Yes, we should," Sarah retorted. "We need him."

"Are you sure?" Sophie asked.

"Am I still here?" Charles asked, looking at first one woman, then the other. "Stop talking about me like I'm not here and tell me what this is all about."

Sarah began talking, and Sophie added details until Charles was caught up on everything the women knew as far as why Andy ran and what Amanda had said. "Here is what we're thinking," Sarah added. "We're thinking about talking Andy into turning himself in. . . ."

"Why would he do that?" Charles asked, "What about his daughter?"

"Okay, that's where we come in. What we want to do is convince Andy that he should turn himself in so that the repercussions of his escape will be minimized and we, with your help, will find Caitlyn."

"Wow. That's a tall order. What makes you think we can find her?" Charles asked.

"We have you!" Sarah said with confidence.

Charles closed his eyes tight and rubbed his forehead with both hands while shaking his head. "You have me? Now, tell me, what makes you think I'm willing to get involved in this?"

"Because you care about this lady," Sophie said flipping her outstretched palm toward Sarah.

Charles finally opened his eyes, looked at Sarah and said with a half smile, "Well, that's true." All three were quiet for a while, sipping coffee and sampling the coffee cake which had grown cold but was still tasty. Finally, Charles spoke saying, "Okay, let's give it a try. If, and that's a very big if, *if* Andy is willing to turn himself in and trust us to do the dirty work, I'm in. But if he's still on the loose, I'm out of this. I have no desire to spend any of my remaining years behind bars with you girls."

"Don't worry," Sophie said looking as serious as Sophie was ever able to look. "We'll be at the women's prison planning our escape."

"I don't doubt it," Charles said, again shaking his head as if to say he could hardly believe he was mixed up with these two. "So where's Andy now?" Charles asked.

"Oh no! You can't have it both ways," Sarah said emphatically. "If you don't want to be involved in *harboring*, then you stay out of it until Andy is safely back in custody. Then we'll talk."

Turning to Sophie, Sarah said, "Come on, Sophie. Let's go see what Andy thinks of our plan."

Sarah gave Charles a quick peck on the cheek and said, "Lock up when you leave, please. Oh, and will you take Barney for a walk?" Without waiting for an answer, Sarah and Sophie were out the door and hurrying to the car. Again, Charles shook his head in wonderment.

Chapter 6

Sarah was exhausted. She had very little sleep the night before and would have loved to sleep in, but today was the second quilt class, and it had been rescheduled to mornings instead of evenings. Ruth usually did classes after the shop closed, but she was excited about the sampler quilt and wanted her customers to be able to see the class in action.

The classroom was at the back of the store but was divided only by a half wall; customers were able to watch without causing much disturbance. "I'd like to see your Log Cabin blocks before we go on to the next block," Ruth announced. Everyone pulled their blocks out and laid them on their work tables. Everyone, that is, except Dottie.

"I wasn't able to finish mine," she announced in a somewhat whiny tone. "The kids just wouldn't leave me alone." She pulled out the logs that she had cut, but nothing had been sewn.

"I see your six light logs, Dottie, but I only see four dark logs," Ruth said.

"I ran out of material," Dottie offered. "I had enough when I started, but I must have made some mistakes cutting. Or maybe I lost them. Can I get more of this one?"

"Sure," Ruth said, "but please do that after class."

"But I wanted to finish it today," Dottie complained.

"We're going on to the next block, Dottie. Please work on today's project along with the class and finish your first block at home. If you need help with it, you can stop in the shop and I'll help you." Dottie looked displeased but nodded. The barrette, which had been struggling to hold back her mass of red curls, flew off. Dottie climbed under the table to retrieve it, knocking her tote bag over in the process. Five marbles rolled across the floor.

"Those kids!" Dottie grumbled.

Ruth looked at the other blocks and was pleased to see that everyone else had finished theirs. "Did you measure your blocks and square them up?" Everyone nodded yes. "When we start putting our blocks together, you'll see why this is so important."

Sarah stifled a yawn. She hadn't been able to sleep the night before. She was worried about Andy. Now that she and Sophie had a plan, she was eager to get started. She was especially eager to get Charles involved, but she needed to get Andy to agree to turn himself in. The problem was Andy was nowhere to be found.

She and Sophie went to the motel where he said he was staying, but he had checked out. They had no way to reach him; they had no idea where he might have gone. They would just have to wait until they heard from him again. In the meantime, if the police picked him up as an escaped convict, he would serve the maximum term, and it could be years before he could connect with his daughter.

"Okay, let's get started on this week's block," Ruth was saying. Sarah set her worries aside and gave Ruth her full attention. "Today's block is the monkey wrench. This is a very easy block and for the newer quilters, it will give you a chance to learn an easy way to make half-square triangles." Pointing to the quilt, Ruth added, "You'll see one in each corner of the monkey wrench." They were squares divided diagonally into two triangles.

"How was this block used to communicate with the runaways?" Danny asked.

"Good question, Danielle," Ruth responded, but noticed the young woman was frowning. "Oh, I'm sorry. I forgot you prefer to be called Danny." Now the grandmother was frowning. Ruth decided to ignore the exchange and went on to explain. "It's suspected that the monkey wrench, being a tool, may have been a way of saying that it was time to pack up and get ready to leave. Again, no one knows for sure." Danny smiled and nodded her thank you.

Everyone finished their block during the class this time. Even Dottie. Ruth suggested they each put their two finished blocks up on the design wall just to get a feel for what it was going to look like finished.

"They don't look too good side by side," Sarah noted.

"Yes, but look at the quilt on the wall. There will be a two-inch strip between each block. That's called *sashing*. Maybe you should start thinking about what fabric you'll want for your sashing." Although Ruth didn't say it, Sarah knew she should choose her border fabric first to ensure that the sashing was compatible. She had enjoyed the class and had, momentarily, forgotten about Andy and his problems.

* * * * *

When Sarah returned home, she went into the sewing room, opened the oak cabinet where she kept her fabric and again looked at the bottom shelf.

Still empty! "What did I expect?" she said aloud.

Andy's quilt wasn't there the previous week when she and Sophie went in to get it; it wasn't there yesterday or this morning when she checked again.

What could possibly have happened to it?

Sophie thought Sarah had misplaced it, but Sarah knew exactly where she put it. It had been on the bottom shelf of her oak cabinet since the day Andy gave it to her. Nevertheless, she searched all the other storage spots in the house, knowing full well she hadn't put it in any of those places.

Sarah knew she should tell Charles it was missing, but she hesitated to involve him. She realized that the only possibility was that someone had been in the house, and that would certainly upset Charles.

And why hadn't Barney stopped the person?

As before, she closed the cabinet and shook her head. *What could have happened to it?* Sarah sat down on the futon and thought about the first time she heard about Andy's tie quilt. She had met Andy just outside her house and she told him she was planning to make a quilt with her husband's ties. He got excited and told her about the tie quilt his grandmother had made using his father's old ties. That night, he left the tie quilt at Sarah's house for her to look at it but, unfortunately, that was the night his brother, George, turned up at Andy's house demanding the quilt. This led to the fight which resulted in George's death and, ultimately, Andy's incarceration. George had told Andy there was something sewn into the quilt which would lead to family money. Andy didn't really believe the story but hadn't had a chance to check it out before he was arrested.

In the meantime, Sarah still had the quilt. Or, at least, she *did* have the quilt. Now it was gone. Sarah sighed, turned off the light, and got ready for bed.

I'll have to tell Andy it's gone. He'll be devastated!

Chapter 7

Sarah had just finished her third class and still no word from Andy. Ruth had seemed distracted all through the class, and Katie had done much of the teaching. They'd started their third block, the Bear Paw. Ruth didn't offer any history about the block, but during the break Katie reminded them that Ruth had previously talked about it. "Some think it was designed as a message to the runaways to follow the bear tracks in order to get through the mountains," she said. "But others say it probably meant to follow the tracks to water. At least, it was a pretty clear sign to follow the bear's tracks!" she said with a smile. Sarah noticed that Katie had been watching her mother attentively throughout the class.

After their class, Sarah joined Ruth in the kitchenette where Ruth was making a cup of tea. "Will you join me?" she asked Sarah.

"I'd love to," Sarah responded. "Are you okay? You seem distracted today."

"Oh, I'm okay, Sarah," Ruth said halfheartedly. "My brother called last night and told me my father is seriously ill. I'm just trying to decide what to do."

"Are you thinking about going to Ohio?" Sarah asked. She knew Ruth had been out of touch with her family since she left home many years before. Her family was Amish, and Ruth described her father as *old world* and very strict. He was extremely upset when Ruth married outside the Amish faith and had cut her off from the family.

"I don't want to upset them by attempting to visit, but I'd love to be there for my mother right now. I'm just not sure what to do. I haven't been home for over twenty years."

"What about the shop? Would you close for a few days?"

"Katie can handle it. She knows as much as I do about running the shop, and I should only be gone two or three days. And Nathan can always come in for a few hours if she needs him," Ruth added with a smile. Nathan Weaver was Ruth's husband. They'd been married for many years; yet they behaved like newlyweds. Sarah was always reminded of her own marriage whenever she was around them. She and Jonathan had had that same kind of loving relationship. She still smiled when she thought of him even though he had been gone for nearly twenty years. *It doesn't seem possible.*

"Oops! Look at the time!" Sarah said abruptly. "I was supposed to meet Sophie at the cafe ten minutes ago! Gotta run. Let me know if you get any news about your father and if there's anything I can do to help," she added as she gave Ruth a hug and hurried out the door.

As she entered the cafe across the street from Stitches, Sophie waved to her from the back. She was already settled in their favorite booth and was enjoying a steaming latte piled high with whipped cream. "Hi. Sorry I'm late."

"No problem, kiddo." Sophie was wearing her purple running suit, although she never ran, and her comfortable walking shoes, although she rarely walked. She had taken the bus to the cafe so she could ride home with Sarah. "Where's your quilting bag? I wanted to see today's block."

"Oh! I left it in the shop. We can stop in there after lunch."

They both ordered burgers and fries and chatted about this and that through lunch. Sophie asked what classes Sarah was going to sign up for this year at the center. Sophie never took classes but was always interested in hearing what Sarah was doing.

Sarah had taken several computer classes but was now using the computer lab on her own. She signed up for a swimming class but just couldn't get the hang of it. Truth be known, and she rarely admitted it, she was afraid of deep water. She had dropped out of the class when they moved to the deep end and, instead, enrolled in water aerobics which she loved.

"I don't know, Sophie. I haven't been over to check the schedule."

"Well, I was talking to a bunch of women in the coffee shop the other day, and they were all planning to sign up for the hula hoop class!" Sophie scrunched her face up and, shaking her head, added, "Can you just see that bunch of old ladies trying to get that hoop going?"

Sarah laughed heartily and teased Sophie by saying, "And did you sign up?"

"Sign up!" Sophie squealed. "Do you really think that hoop would fit over this body?"

"Now, Sophie! You aren't *that* big, and you know it. I think it would be fun."

"Well, then, my dear, you go right ahead and do it. It's certainly not for me!"

Although they were just joking at first, Sarah found herself giving it some serious consideration. "It actually does sound like fun and great exercise. I just might give it a try."

"Humph," Sophie responded.

Turning to a more serious topic, Sophie said, "I'm getting very worried about Andy. Do you think he might have been arrested?"

"I just don't know, Sophie. I'm worried. He doesn't know we talked to Charles and have a plan to help him. He has gone off on his own to find Caitlyn, and there's no way to guess where he is or what he's doing. He might've contacted Buck, but we don't know Buck's last name or how to find him."

"Buck?"

"Caitlyn's stepfather," Sarah responded. "The man Catherine married instead of Andy."

"Ah yes. Maybe Charles could find him?" Sophie suggested.

"I don't know. Charles made it pretty clear he didn't want to have any part of this until Andy was back in prison. We have to respect that."

"You're right. Maybe we should talk to Amanda. Do you think we could trust her to help us?" Sophie asked.

"Hmm. I don't know. But it's a thought," Sarah said pensively. "Maybe we should wait another week; if we don't hear from Andy by then, let's think about sitting down with Amanda and telling her what we know. I'm curious about that quilt, too, and I wonder if I should be reporting it as a break-in. For some reason, I just don't think that's what it was. Who would come in and take just that quilt and nothing else? And who would know where it was kept? And who would know where the door key was hidden?"

"Andy!" Sophie announced abruptly, her eyes wide open, and her eyebrows raised high on her forehead. "Andy would know all those things!"

"*Andy?* No! That's not possible!" Sarah said emphatically. The two women remained quiet for a few seconds. Sarah began to frown and added, "But why would he take it when all he had to do was ask for it? And, for that matter, *when* would he have taken it?" Sarah asked searching Sophie's face for an answer.

"Maybe after we talked to him by the river. Or, maybe before that," Sophie suggested.

"Before?" Sarah gasped. "You mean he may have been in my house before he contacted me?"

"He may have been in your house before we even knew he was out of prison!"

Sarah was stunned and clearly shaken by the idea. She suddenly felt very vulnerable. "Can we trust Andy?"

Sophie grimaced as she shook her head and quietly said, "I just don't know anymore."

"We don't have any concrete reason to suspect Andy of breaking into my house, but we do know that he needs our help. And I think the best help we can offer is for us to take over the job of looking for Caitlyn and for us to convince him to turn himself in. But we can't do any of these things until we find him. We need Amanda's help."

As they were getting up from the table, Sarah said, "Okay. It's decided. We will contact Amanda next week and see if she'll help us find him."

Once outside, they decided to walk up the street to the craft shop. "I've been wanting to find a little gift for Ruth. She does so much for her students, and her father is ill. I think she needs a little something special."

As they approached the shop, Sophie asked, "Why do you suppose they named this shop Persnickety Place?"

"I don't know," Sarah shrugged. "Let's ask." They entered the shop and walked past a line of wind chimes that responded with clinks and clatters as the breeze hit them. To the left, Sophie spotted a room spilling over with Christmas items.

"Oh look! My favorites!" she called to Sarah.

"You go on in the Christmas room." Sarah said. "I'm going to look for a little something for Ruth." Walking farther into the shop, Sarah was overwhelmed by all the wonderful items. She saw quilts, jewelry, handbags, scarves, and all sorts of small fun items. "I could spend all afternoon in here," she muttered to herself.

"Feel free to do just that," a woman was saying as she entered the room. "And when you finish, meet me out front for ice cream!"

"Are you the owner?" Sarah asked.

"Yes, this is my shop. I'm Bea. And you are … ?"

"I'm Sarah. I'm taking a quilting class up the street and have wanted to stop in. It's a fascinating building. Do you know its history?"

"As a matter of fact, I do. It was built in 1835 and was originally just a two-room log cabin. The original owners were very poor but were able to save up and build on to it in 1850 and, by 1870, they were able to add the upstairs. It passed through several hands until it finally got to me about twelve years ago." She smiled and looked around the room with pride. Sarah could see that Bea had a special love for the building and her shop.

While Sophie entertained herself in the Christmas room, Sarah and Bea relaxed in rocking chairs and continued to talk. Sarah enjoyed getting to know Bea and appreciated that Bea took the time to sit and visit with her.

Calling to Sophie, Bea said, "Let me know if I can help you." Then she added, "By the way, everything in that room is 50% off!"

"Oh, wonderful!" the voice from the Christmas room cried out.

Sarah returned to her shopping and ultimately settled on a small bag which Ruth could carry in her purse or use for her small sewing items. Sophie came toward the cash register with an armload of furry snowmen, sleigh bells, and sparkling tree decorations.

As they were leaving the shop, Sophie stopped abruptly and demanded, "What about the ice cream?"

They turned back to the shop and Bea scooped extra-large, delicious cones which they enjoyed leisurely while sitting in the shop's outdoor gazebo.

"Let's not wait," Sophie said suddenly. "We need to talk to Amanda today. I have a bad feeling about Andy."

Using Sarah's cell phone, they called Officer Holmes from the gazebo. Amanda told them she was on her way out but could meet them the next morning. Sarah, wanting to keep the meeting informal, asked her to meet them on the north end of the park. That was only a few minutes from their house and Sophie would be able to walk there.

The two friends walked back to the quilt shop where Sarah's car was parked, picked up Sarah's quilt supplies, and headed home, both feeling hopeful and apprehensive at the same time.

Chapter 8

The next morning, Sarah and Sophie walked over to the park. They found a table and sat down. The sun was warm on their faces. Squirrels were scampering up and down the trees, perhaps searching for last year's hidden stash of nuts. A few minutes later, Amanda pulled up in a squad car and joined them.

"Thank you for seeing us, Officer Holmes."

"No problem. What's up?" Amanda was a lovely young woman, about thirty-two years old with short brown hair and deep brown eyes. She had joined the police department the previous year and was assigned to Detective Gabriel. Amanda had worked closely with Sarah and Sophie during the investigation that ultimately led to Andy's arrest the previous year. Amanda was a quilter and Sarah felt they were becoming friends. "And call me Amanda," the officer added with a smile.

"Okay, Amanda," Sarah began. "We're really going out on a limb here. We hope we can trust you with what we're going to tell you."

"I'll do the best I can. I know how you gals feel about Andy and, to tell the truth, I found him to be a very gentle and caring guy myself. I find it hard to understand some of the things he does. Do you know why he ran off this time?"

This time? During the fight with his brother, George had fallen back against the fireplace and died. Instead of facing an investigation which would probably have cleared him of any wrongdoing, Andy ran off to Florida, letting all his friends think he was dead. And now, worried about his daughter, he ran off from the prison farm. *Even his drinking was a way of running away from his problems.* "... and now his daughter is running ..." Sarah said aloud.

"What?" Amanda asked, puzzled by the comment.

"Sorry. I was just thinking."

"Well, stop thinking," Sophie demanded, "and start talking. We have this young lady's attention."

Sarah told Amanda everything that Andy had told them about Catherine, Caitlyn, Buck, and why he took off from the prison. Sophie interjected at every turn which seemed to confuse Amanda more than help her to understand the story. "What hobo camp?" Amanda asked at one point.

"That isn't important to the story, Amanda." Turning to Sophie, she added, "Please, Sophie, let's just give her the facts so she can help us decide where to go from here."

"I was just trying to help," Sophie snorted. "And what about the quilt?"

"What quilt?" Amanda asked, again looking perplexed.

"No. Again, that isn't our main concern right now. What we want to do is find Andy, and tell him that we will look for Caitlyn if he'll turn himself in. That will work in his favor, right?"

"Yes. As I told you before, if he turns himself in, I'll recommend to the district attorney that he be given leniency because of turning himself in and because of his daughter."

"And that will help him, right?"

"I can't guarantee it, but the prison staff will vouch for his good behavior, and you two can testify about the daughter. It will certainly help his case if he comes in voluntarily and not in cuffs."

"So," Sarah began. "We want to find Andy and we want to find Caitlyn. Where do you think we should start?"

"Well," Amanda began. "You suspect the girl might be on the streets in Hamilton. Has she been reported missing?"

"I have no idea, but I doubt it," Sarah responded.

"Well, that's something I can do. I'll check with Hamilton Missing Persons and see if they're looking for her. What's her name?"

"I don't know. Andy just called her Caitlyn."

"Okay. I'll find out and let you know. I can't get involved with searching for her—that's out of my jurisdiction. Now, Sarah, you need to understand that the police are looking for Andy. If they pick him up, there's nothing I can do to help him. The best case scenario for him will be if he turns himself in voluntarily. If he agrees to do that, call me and I'll help him through the system."

"Thank you, Amanda. We appreciate your candor and your help. We'll talk to Andy and see if he's willing to turn himself in if we promise to search for Caitlyn."

"How do you propose to do that?" Amanda asked.

"I honestly don't know, but Charles has offered to help us once Andy is back in jail. He refuses to have anything to do with it until then."

"I understand. Okay, ladies. Good luck to you and I'll let you know if the Hamilton Police Department is looking for the girl." Amanda walked back to the squad car and turned to wave as she got in.

"Nice girl," Sophie said. "I like her." Turning to Sarah and looking worried, she added, "What've we gotten ourselves into?"

"It's okay, Sophie. We just need to chip away at the problems. First of all, we need to know Caitlyn's and Buck's last name. Andy would know, but until we hear from him, that's no help."

"I think we should go to Evanston prison farm and talk to *Carrot-top*," Sophie suggested.

"His name is Bryce, but that's all we know about him," Sarah responded.

"Do you suppose they'll let us see him if we don't even know his full name?"

"I'll call Amanda and see if she can get his name for us. He should be able to tell us how to get in touch with this Buck fellow and he might have some ideas about where the girl has gone."

The two women remained sitting in the park. "This police work is exhausting," Sophie announced. "I don't think I can walk home from here. Do you think your cutie-pie would pick us up?"

"I'll give him a call. I think we can tell him about talking to Amanda. That doesn't involve him."

"Do you think he could pick us up at that little shop? I could use an ice cream cone," Sophie said timidly.

"Of course, he will! We'll even buy one for him." Although much too tired to walk home, Sophie enthusiastically led the way across the park and up the street to the ice cream shop.

* * * * *

By the time Charles dropped Sarah off at home, she was feeling emotionally exhausted. Charles had pointed out to the women that they shouldn't lean on Amanda for too much help and inside information as it could jeopardize her position in the department. Sarah hadn't thought of that and resolved to leave Amanda out of their planning.

From the time she first met Amanda, she couldn't help but compare her to her own daughter, Martha. Amanda was upbeat, enthusiastic about her job, and seemed to love life. Martha, on the other hand, wore despair on her face. She rarely smiled, had no close friends that Sarah knew of and spent all of her time in the laboratory. She was a scientist doing work which she refused to discuss with Sarah; perhaps it was classified, or perhaps she just didn't want to share it with her mother. At any rate, Sarah took an immediate liking to Amanda and hoped their friendship could continue to grow once all these crimes were out of the way.

Sarah checked the answering machine, poured herself a glass of tea, and decided to soak in a deep bubble bath.

Barney pushed the bathroom door open with his nose and looked at Sarah whose head was protruding from a mass of bubbles. "Woof?" Barney said questioningly.

"I know, dear dog," she said with a chuckle. "Why would anyone submerge them self in a tub of water voluntarily?" Barney curled up against the tub protectively and rested his head on his paws.

Chapter 9

"This is our fourth class and you gals are doing a great job!" Ruth was placing all the finished blocks on the design wall. Ruth looked particularly relaxed. Sarah suspected that she may have decided what she would do about her family. She didn't want to intrude on her privacy, but decided she would hang around after class and see if Ruth wanted to talk.

"I have mine right here," Dottie said proudly as she searched through her tote bag and finally located the rumpled block.

Ruth smiled and responded, "Thank you, Dottie. You did a lovely job. I like the colors you've chosen. Having the bear claws in two shades of brown and the background a pale green, it's as if the bear is walking across a meadow. Good choices!" Dottie beamed with pride.

"Which block are we doing today?"

"Let's do something a little different this week. Let's do the *Wagon Wheel*. It will involve using a template to cut the spoke, machine piecing, and then hand appliquéing."

"And the significance of this block?" Kimberly asked.

"I'm not really sure," Ruth responded. "I haven't seen much written about this block but it was certainly common during that period. Maybe it refers to how they'll travel. Some people built their wagons with false bottoms to hide runaways. Or maybe it just meant 'follow the wagon trails,'" she added shrugging. "We'll probably never know, but it's fun to speculate."

Ruth passed out the template for the spokes and told the class to choose their fabrics and begin cutting. Over the next two hours, everyone had their spokes cut out and stitched together in a ring. Ruth then showed them how to hand appliqué the ring to the background and then a circle to the center. Delores, a seasoned quilter, was the only one to make any progress on the appliqué, and Ruth realized this was too much for one class. "Work on this one at home and if you have any trouble just stop by the shop, and Katie or I will help you."

After the class, Sarah pulled a book from the rack and thumbed through it. "Are you considering your next project?" Katie asked.

"I've been thinking about a quilt for my bed. I love florals, but I'm not sure what pattern I will use. Ruth joined them and pulled another book from the rack and flipped through it to a scrap quilt she thought Sarah might like. "It's beautiful," Sarah exclaimed. "But I don't have many scraps yet!"

"You haven't been to the Friday night quilt group at all this month, and we miss you. Why don't you and Barney come this Friday and I'll put the word out that you need scraps. If there's one thing quilters have lots of, it's scraps!"

"Good idea, Ruth! Thanks. I've missed the group too." Over the past year, the group had grown to about fifteen. The previous year they used Ruth's machines, but since the group had grown, they just brought handwork and their projects for *show and tell*, as quilters call it. It was clear that most people came for the socializing and the support of other quilters. "Is it really okay to ask for scraps?" Sarah asked timidly.

"Absolutely! Quilters love to share and are very generous people."

"I'm glad you're still here," Ruth added, lowering her voice so Katie wouldn't hear. "I've decided what to do about my family, and I wanted to tell you since you were so kind to listen to my sniveling last week."

"Nonsense! If we can't snivel with our friends, where can we snivel?"

"Well, it helped me. Just getting the words out helped me to see what I need to do. I'm going to drive up to Ohio and knock on the door. I don't know if they'll see me, but I have to try."

"I think that's a good plan."

"If they're willing to see me, I'll bring Katie next time. I don't have any idea if my father is home or in the hospital. I suspect, if he's home, the family will turn me away, but I'm prepared for that. Shunning is the Amish way of dealing with its members who go against the faith. I've grown up with it, and I understand it. I miss my family, but I understand."

"You're a strong, brave woman, Ruth. I so admire you." Sarah pulled Ruth into a warm hug.

"You are a strong woman yourself, Sarah," Ruth said as she returned the hug.

"What's with this?" Katie teased, entering the room. "If you two are so strong, how about helping me pick up the bolts of fabric scattered all over the shop."

* * * * *

Sarah stopped at the community center on her way home. "Hi, Marjory," Sarah called as she walked into the resource room. The resource room was located on the second floor of the center. The center, itself, looked like an old warehouse from the outside, but it had been gutted and rebuilt as a community center just a few blocks from Sarah's house. The lobby was two stories high and contained tropical plants that nearly reached the skylights.

There was an upper level walkway overlooking the lobby and glass-sided elevators that carried people between the two levels. On the first floor, in addition to the lobby, there were numerous activity rooms. Many had large interior windows revealing the activities which were going on inside. There were exercise and ballet classes and a swimming pool. Sarah remembered her first visit to the community center. She had watched people laughing and cavorting in the pool, their wheelchairs abandoned by the side of the pool. She could imagine their joy at experiencing this freedom.

The upper level was primarily classrooms and the resource room where people signed up for classes. "Sarah, it's good to see you," Marjory said warmly as Sarah walked into the resource room. "Are you thinking about signing up for another class?"

"Well, I'm thinking about it." Sarah responded. "Actually, I want to find out more about something that has tickled my fancy. What's this hula hoop class all about?" Sarah asked, with a shy giggle.

Marjory laughed as she picked up a pile of brochures and pulled one off for Sarah to read. "This will tell you all about it. It sounds like a fun way to get in shape."

"To get in shape?" Sarah responded with surprise.

"Yes, read the brochure and you'll see."

Sarah slipped on her new reading glasses. She was still getting used to using them, but it made life so much easier. She was holding things so far from her face that Sophie suggested she needed longer arms.

The brochure was entitled "Hula Hoop Your Way to Health." Sarah went on to read that *hooping* could strengthen and tone the whole body and improve posture, coordination, and balance. It told about other benefits such as stress reduction and weight loss. There were pictures of men and women of all ages *hooping their way to health.*

"This could be fun," Sarah said enthusiastically. "I just might try it." Both women laughed and mimicked the hooping movement with their arms above their heads.

"Maybe I should think about signing up too," Marjory said excitedly. Sarah took two registration forms, one for herself and one for Sophie. She couldn't imagine how she'd ever talk Sophie into taking hula hoop classes, but she was sure going to try.

On her way home, Sarah wondered briefly if this was how she should be spending her time when there was so much to do to help Andy, but she immediately told herself how important it was to nourish the body and the mind. Sarah smiled as she wondered how she would talk Sophie into joining her.

Chapter 10

There was a message on Sarah's phone but her caller ID
simply said *unknown caller*. She let Barney out in the
backyard before picking it up.

"Hi, Sarah. It's Andy. I'm sorry I took so long contacting
you. It's been a crazy month. I hate this hiding out.
Anyway, you can't call me back, but I have a problem. I'm
out of money, and I don't dare go near my bank. I've been
wondering if George was right and there might be a clue in
that quilt about where my grandfather hid some cash. Would
you check it and see and I'll call back in a day or two."

Obviously, she thought, Andy was not the person who'd
been in her house. At first, Sarah was relieved, but she
immediately realized that meant someone else *had* been in
the house. She called Sophie right away and, again, they
speculated about who it could have been. "I think you need
to tell Amanda about this," Sophie said. "It's more serious
than we originally thought."

"I agree. I'll call her this afternoon." In the meantime,
she picked up the phone to call Charles and tell him about it
but, again, decided against involving him. *He worries enough*

*about me. Knowing someone got into the house would drive
him crazy.*

The phone rang again, and Sarah picked it up on the
first ring, hoping it was Andy. "Hi, Sarah. This is Amanda.
I'm driving right by Cunningham Village and wondered if
I could stop by your house. I have that name you wanted."

"That would be great, Amanda. I have something to talk
about with you, too." Sarah decided she would go ahead and
report the quilt as missing. It was time.

A few minutes later, Amanda knocked on the door.
Barney, as usual, ran to the door and excitedly turned to look
at Sarah to make sure she was going to open it for him. All
guests, he was sure, came only to see him! As Sarah opened
the door, he backed up a few steps, not recognizing the
woman. Immediately, she smiled and held her hand palm
down for him to sniff. He sensed that this was a friendly
person and tried to wag his tail without his entire lower body
wagging, but it was a losing battle. Both women laughed
as Amanda stooped down and wrapped her arms around
his neck. He appeared to swoon in her embrace. He added
another person to his *pack*.

"Hi, Sarah. How's it going?"

"I'm doing fine, but I'm eager to hear what you've found
out."

"And you had something you wanted to talk to me
about?" Amanda asked.

"Yes, but you go first. Have you found out anything about
the girl or Andy?"

"I got Carrot-top's name for you. It's Bryce Silverman.
He's in for some minor brawling. I'm not thrilled that you
two are planning a visit to the prison, but you might get

more information out of him than the police would. And he sounds like an okay guy. He shouldn't cause you any trouble."

"Great. Thanks, Amanda. And how about Caitlyn? Are the Hamilton police looking for her?" Sarah asked eagerly.

"They don't have a missing person's report on her. Once we find out who this Buck guy is, we can get him to file a report."

"Andy's her father. Can't he report her?" Sarah asked.

"No. Legally, Buck is her father until the courts say otherwise."

The two women spent another hour in the kitchen sipping coffee and talking about family and quilts. Sarah pulled out the blocks she was working on and a picture of the completed sampler quilt.

As they talked, Amanda said she would like to start coming to the Friday night group again on a regular basis. "I really enjoyed the people. There are some very talented quilters there, and they inspired me to pull out my stash and consider sewing again. There's just so little time," she added regretfully.

"You just have to make the time. We all need time to rest, relax, play, and express our creative side. It can't all be work."

"I don't know that I have a creative side," Amanda said.

"We all have one!" Sarah responded. "We just have to take the time to find it. Do you do anything that you just get lost in where time passes, and you're hardly aware of where you are or what you've been doing?" Sarah asked.

"Yes. That happens when I'm designing a quilt!"

"See?"

"Oh, also when I'm hand quilting. The up and down motion of the needle lulls me into a very peaceful place."

"Okay, so there you have relaxation and creativity all in one activity. So … do you think you can make the time to get quilting back into your life?"

"Yes!" Amanda said emphatically, slapping the table top. "I'll do just that." They both laughed.

As the two women were walking toward the front door, Amanda turned suddenly and asked, "Didn't you want to talk to me about something?" Sarah had enjoyed the time she and Amanda had spent together so much that she didn't want to ruin it. She decided to talk about the disappearing quilt another day.

"Yes, but it wasn't important and we'll talk about it another time."

Amanda looked at her questioningly. "Are you sure?" Amanda asked with a slight frown.

"Absolutely." She touched Amanda's arm and said, "It was fun visiting with you today. I sure hope you decide to come to the quilt group. And just think how happy it will make Barney!" Barney had become a regular member of the Friday night quilt group.

* * * * *

"And *why* didn't you tell Amanda about the robbery?" Sophie asked, using her most disapproving tone.

"It's hard to explain, Sophie. Amanda is just such a sweet girl, and I love spending time with her. It's like having a daughter."

"You already have a daughter," Sophie said, still using the disapproving tone.

"Oh, Sophie. I know. It's just different. It's hard to explain."

"Well, kiddo. You have to remember that relationships take two people. Martha can't be all to blame if things aren't working out for the two of you."

"I do everything I can!" Sarah retorted indignantly.

"Bull feathers."

"What do you mean?" Sarah demanded.

"You're as stubborn as she is. And this conversation isn't for you and me to have. Go talk to your daughter." Sophie headed for the kitchen, clearly ending the conversation.

Feeling very annoyed with Sophie, Sarah picked up their tea cups and the leftover cookies and carried them into the kitchen. Sophie was warming up the tea kettle so obviously wasn't planning to leave right away. Sarah set the cups on the kitchen table along with the cookies and two clean plates. "I'm sorry, Sophie," she finally said. "I shouldn't get defensive. I could do more to mend the fences with Martha, I guess. I just don't know what the problem is."

"I should mind my own business," Sophie began, "... but if you want my opinion ..." Sarah clearly didn't, but Sophie went on, "... you two need to talk and not about the weather! You need to talk about the problem. Yell, scream, get it out in the open."

"We never do that," Sarah said quietly.

"I know you don't. But until you do, it will just continue to lay there between you two like a big dead rooster."

"A big dead rooster?" Sarah repeated, laughing. Sophie laughed too and the tension was relieved. They drank their third cup of tea and talked about what they would do next.

"I think we need to go see this Buck fellow, and we can't do that until we know where he lives," Sarah said.

"True," Sophie said, sipping her tea. "So, we need to go see this carrot-topped guy, right?"

"Right. Tomorrow I'll call the prison and see when visiting hours are," Sarah offered.

"Why not call now?" Sophie asked.

"Now? It's 9:30 at night," Sarah said raising her eyebrows questioningly. "Do you think … ?"

"Do I think they're closed for the night?" Sophie responded sarcastically. "No, I don't think the prison closes. Give it a try."

Sarah dialed the number Amanda had given her and there was an immediate answer. "Yeah?" the man said.

"Could you tell me your visiting hours please?" Sarah asked politely, feeling a bit intimidated by the man who'd answered rather gruffly."

"Two 'til four every day," the man responded and hung up.

"Well, I was going to ask for directions, but I guess we can use Charles' GPS," Sarah suggested.

"I thought it was yours. Didn't Charles buy that for you?"

"Yes, but I prefer to think of it as his. It doesn't like me very much. The voice and I got off to a rocky start," Sarah replied.

"Do you want to go tomorrow?" Sophie asked.

"Yes, let's get this done. I'll ask Charles to program the monster in the morning, and we can leave about noon. That will give us plenty of time to get there."

"It's a plan," Sophie said as she stood up to leave. Barney followed her to the door and attempted to go with her.

"See? He loves you!" Sarah remarked.

"Humph."

Sarah grabbed the leash and she and Barney walked Sophie to her door, then on up the street for a little exercise. "I have to leave you alone again tomorrow," she told Barney apologetically as they walked. "Would you like to go stay with Charles?" Barney wagged his tail when he heard Charles' name.

The next morning, Sarah called Charles and arranged to stop by and get the GPS programmed to the prison and leave Barney for a visit.

As Sarah and Sophie approached the prison, they both became apprehensive. "Have you ever been inside a prison?" Sophie asked.

"No, but I don't think this is like a typical prison. Andy told me the security is very loose. He said the men here aren't career criminals or dangerous," Sarah explained. Andy had been doing farm work when he first arrived, growing food that was used mainly in the facility. But, when they learned about his computer skills, they assigned him to the lab as a computer instructor. "He didn't sound like it was too bad serving his time here," she added.

"How about this Silverman guy," Sophie asked. "What's he in for?"

"Amanda said it was something minor. Let's just hope he's willing to talk to us."

As the guard led Silverman into the visitor's room, he stopped and looked at first one and then the other woman. "I don't know you!" he exclaimed. "Are you two *my* visitors?"

"Yes," Sarah spoke up. "We're hoping you can help us."

"I doubt it. I don't even know you," Silverman said as he walked toward the table where they were sitting. He took a seat across the table from the two women and looked first at Sophie then at Sarah. "So … ?"

"We're friends of Andy Burgess," Sarah began.

"Stop right there!" Silverman said standing up. "If the cops sent you in here to get information out of me, you can all forget it. The man was an idiot to walk off when he probably would have been out of here in a few months. But I won't help you people find him, even if he *is* an idiot."

"That's not it, Bryce. May I call you Bryce?" Sarah asked.

"Whatever …" the carrot-topped man replied.

"I'm Sarah and this is my friend Sophie. We're Andy's friends. We're trying to help him find his daughter and we think you can help."

"Daughter? Andy doesn't have a daughter," Silverman responded, sitting back down.

"Please wait, Bryce. Andy had a daughter with Catherine. She married Buck. You know them all. Buck threw the girl out after Catherine left him, and we're trying to help Andy find her."

Sitting back down and looking interested, "Well, I'll be horsewhipped! Is that why Andy left here?"

"That's exactly why he left."

"What makes you think I can help? I don't know the girl."

"We know. But you know Buck. We don't know how to find him, and we think he could give us a lead as to where Caitlyn might have gone. We're hoping you could tell us his last name and, possibly, where we can find him."

"Why doesn't Andy tell you that stuff?"

"We saw Andy once. He let us know what he's doing so we wouldn't worry, but then he disappeared. We can't reach him, but we want to help by finding Caitlyn before the police find him. Will you help us?" Sarah pleaded.

"Heck fire. Andy's a good guy. If the cops pick him up, he won't see the light of day in this lifetime. Buck's name is Buckley. I think his first name is Dan, maybe Daniel, but everyone calls him Buck. He hangs out at that biker bar on the east side. Hogs & Heifers, I think it's called. But gals, don't go there alone. That's one tough hangout."

"We were hoping to go to his house. Do you know where he lives?"

"No, I don't know the man other than having a beer with him and the guys now and then. We used to play poker with him, but he's too mean even for us. You gals be careful." After a short pause, Silverman added, "What's with Andy and this kid, anyway?"

Sarah and Sophie stayed another twenty minutes talking with Bryce and telling him what Andy had confided in them about the child. Sarah didn't think Andy would mind since Silverman was helping them to find her. As they were leaving, he turned and looked at the woman with a very serious look on his face. "I mean it, gals. You be careful around that guy. He's a mean one, he is. It wouldn't surprise me if he's left a body or two behind."

As they walked back to their car, Sophie sighed and said, "What're we getting ourselves into, Sarah? Maybe we should leave this up to Andy."

"The police will find him before he finds Caitlyn. We both know that. He's almost seventy years old. He'll die in prison. He deserves better."

Sophie took a deep breath and let it out slowly. "You're right." As they drove home, they decided to simply check the telephone book, and, if they don't have any luck, they'd ask Amanda to track down his address. But they wouldn't go near the biker bar.

Chapter 11

Sarah and Sophie arrived at Daniel Buckley's house in the early afternoon. The drive to Hamilton was uneventful, and Sophie was unusually quiet. They'd decided to arrive around 1:00 p.m., figuring that would be late enough for Buck to recover from the previous night's hangover, yet early enough that he probably wouldn't be too drunk yet.

The house was run down and weeds overran the yard, obstructing the walkway. As they started up the stairs to the porch, one step screeched as if it were about to collapse under Sophie's weight. She quickly hopped to the next step and onto the porch. The paint on both the porch and house was chipping, and the screen door was ripped. The shade on the front window was hanging askew. They pushed the doorbell but didn't hear a sound.

"It must be broken," Sophie said. "Just knock."

Sarah opened the screen door and knocked. There was no response. After a few minutes, she knocked again. "Awright. Awright. Give me a chance to get my pants on," the angry voice snarled. Opening the door in a dirty undershirt and pants he was still zipping up, Daniel Buckley demanded angrily, "*What!*"

Sarah introduced herself and Sophie. "We're looking for Caitlyn. We were wondering if you could tell us where she might be."

"What business is it of yours?" Buckley snarled.

"We are …" Sarah began, not sure where to go from there.

"We're from the school," Sophie snapped without looking at Sarah. "She's been absent for several weeks, and we're here to find out why. She's required to attend, you know," she said in her most official voice. "Is she here?"

"No! She's not here and she's not welcome here," he growled and slammed the door.

"The school?" Sarah said, glaring at Sophie. "Why would you say that?"

"It's the only way we're going to get any information. Do you have a better idea?"

Sarah hesitantly said, "No. Not really."

"Okay then. Knock again and louder this time … wait, I'll do it." Sophie moved toward the door, opened the screen, took off her shoe, and used it to bang on the door.

"*What do you think you're doing?*" the man yelled as he jerked the door open, now holding a beer.

"I'll ask again," Sophie said, softly this time and with a smile. "Is Caitlyn here?"

"No, and I don't know where she is. And I don't *care* where she is." He, too, spoke more softly, but with a mocking tone and a sneer.

"Okay," Sophie said. "I understand that you don't care where she is, but, since you're her legal guardian, have you reported her missing to the police?"

"No. Why would I do that? I don't want her back."

"You wouldn't like for her to come back home?" Sarah asked, trying to connect with a shred of fatherly concern.

"Home? This isn't her home," he hollered. "And if you find her, don't bring her here. I didn't want nothin' to do with that kid even when I thought she was mine. She's nothin' to me."

"When you *thought* she was yours? Isn't she yours?" Sarah asked, sounding astounded. Of course, she knew Caitlyn was not his daughter, but she didn't know Buck knew it.

"Her mother told me she wasn't mine," Buck said, looking away from the women and seemed a bit sorrowful. They didn't respond and, after a minute or so, his nasty tone returned. "I told her she would never see the kid again if she ran off. Then she told me the kid wasn't even mine anyway. I didn't believe her at first, but I found out for sure." His tone had softened somewhat and he lit a cigarette.

"How did you find out for sure?" Sarah asked.

"I dragged the kid down to the Health Department and had a test. She's not mine. She probably belongs to that criminal Cat used to be with." His combative tone returned and his face twisted with emotion.

Anger? Pain? Regret? Sarah wondered.

"She isn't mine and I'm glad. Not my kid. Not my problem." Buck drank the rest of his beer in one swallow and tossed the can into the yard. He took a long drag on his cigarette and flicked the rest beyond the porch. He watched it land near the beer can. When he looked up, his eyes had softened somewhat, and he asked, "Why do you care?"

"We're trying to find her to make sure she's safe. Would you be willing to call the police and report her missing? We could sure use their help."

The temporary softness was gone and he bellowed, "Absolutely not! I want nothin' to do with the cops. Just leave me out of this." He turned toward the door and Sarah could tell they weren't going to get any help from Buckley. She could see why Caitlyn didn't want to live with this man once her mother was gone.

Before he got the door closed, Sophie asked one more question, hoping they might get a lead on where to find her. "Have you heard from Catherine?"

"Are you kidding?" Buckley exploded, turning to face the women again. "I'd better not hear from that good-fer-nothin' bitch." His face twisted into an angry snarl, and his fists were clinched. Sarah and Sophie knew it was time to leave. They turned and quickly walked toward their car.

"Perhaps they're both better off away from this man," Sarah muttered as they approached their car. Buck continued to stand in front of the house until they drove away.

"Okay," Sophie asked, "What next?"

* * * * *

"You did *what*?" Charles bellowed. Sarah had never seen him this upset. "I can't believe you two women would go anywhere near that man alone after what Silverman told you about him."

"Charles, please. Calm down. We were very careful. We went during the day and we stayed outside and talked to him on the porch. I thought we'd get farther as two women simply trying to help Caitlyn. And turn around! I don't want to talk to your back." Sarah could feel herself getting flushed.

"And did you get anywhere?" Charles asked, a bit sarcastically. He did, however, turn around and face her.

"No," she said in a defensive tone. "No, but I'm not sorry we went, and I don't think he would have talked with us at all if you'd been there."

Sarah was not happy that she found herself defending her actions to Charles. She had been on her own for over twenty years and, she felt, had made pretty good decisions for herself. She didn't want to go into it with Charles right now, but she knew the subject would need to be discussed if they were to continue to be friends.

Sarah knew their friendship was developing into something more and, if that was the case, there needed to be clear ground rules. She was a very strong, independent woman. She realized that Charles' career had required that he present himself as decisive and in control, but that was not what Sarah wanted in a relationship.

They stared into each other's eyes for a few moments, both looking ready for a fight, but suddenly he dropped his eyes and softly said, "I'm sorry, hon. I didn't mean to go off on you. I was just scared. I don't ever want anything to happen to you. I don't want to lose you. Not ever."

"I care about you, too, Charles. But you have to understand that I won't be wrapped in tissue and put on the shelf for safe keeping. I live my life and I'm not accustomed to asking permission. But if it helps you, I can tell you that I value my life and that I'm extremely careful and don't take unnecessary chances. But I'm also not a shrinking violet. And I can't believe that's even what you would want."

"You're right," he said with a smile. "I love you for the woman you are." They were both silent for a few seconds.

The word *love* hadn't made its way into their previous conversations. Sarah wasn't sure what to do with it.

Instead of words, she touched his cheek gently and smiled. He returned her smile and nodded his head almost imperceptibly. "We'll be fine," he said gently pulled her into his arms, holding her close.

She laid her head on his chest and said, just as gently, "Yes, we will."

Chapter 12

"Today's block is called the Bow Tie block and I'm sure you'll find it very easy to complete. We're going to make four small Bow Tie blocks and set them together in a four patch like the one you see here," Ruth said as she pointed to the block on the sample quilt. "It's speculated that this block was used to reminded fugitive slaves to wear proper dress when they were walking through towns so they wouldn't stand out. I've read that ties and other clothing were often provided at the various stations along the trail."

Ruth went on to say, "But I want you to remember that there's no written proof of quilts being used as secret codes. Some historians say it is simply a myth. I believe it's true, but I guess I want to believe it, being a quilter. I'd like to think our predecessors devised such an ingenious scheme."

The group talked about the Underground Railroad and speculated about the possible ways quilts could have been used. Everyone in the class wanted the stories to be true.

"Okay. Let's start." The class was becoming quite proficient at cutting and stitching accurately and, as predicted, everyone finished early. Again, they put all their blocks on the design board and stood back to admire them.

A design board. That's what I need in my sewing room, Sarah thought. She made a mental note to ask Charles to help her figure out a way to hang it. She decided to stop at the craft shop on her way home and purchase a few yards of felt and an extra-large piece of foam board. After class she told Ruth about her plan. "I have an extra foam board in the back," Ruth said and went back to get it. "This is leftover from one of my projects. You are welcome to take it; it's just taking up room here."

"Thank you, Ruth," Sarah said happily. "Now, all I will need is the felt."

"I don't use felt," Ruth responded. "I use a piece of cotton batting. I think it works even better than felt. I spray the foam board with spray adhesive and just smooth it on. It works great."

"I have a big piece of batting left over from the table runner. I'll use that! Thanks so much for your help, Ruth."

"Always glad to help! I wanted to talk to you anyway," Ruth added. "I'm going to drive to Ohio on Tuesday. I decided it would be better to go during the week so Katie won't be inundated with customers. Thursday is class day, but she can handle that too. I'm not sure how long I'll be gone."

"Did you tell her where you're going?" Sarah asked.

"Yes, but only after her father convinced me I should. Nathan thought that she should go with me, but I have no idea what'll happen there. It could be devastating for her, and that's not the way I want her to meet her extended family."

"That makes sense." Sarah responded. "Good luck with this. Take your cell phone and call me from the road if you need to talk."

Ruth gave Sarah a hug and thanked her. Sarah left the shop pleased that she was making headway on Charles' quilt. She realized that she would need to make a few extra blocks in order to make the quilt large enough for his bed. She didn't actually know how big his bed was. *I'm sure not going to ask for a tour of his bedroom.*

* * * * *

When Sarah got home, she immediately dialed Amanda's cell phone. She wanted to tell her about their meeting with Daniel Buckley. "I'm glad you called," Amanda said when she answered. "I knew you were going to talk to Buckley this week, and I was wondering how it went."

"It didn't go well. We didn't find out much of anything. He's just as everyone describes him: a very angry, belligerent man who doesn't seem to care about anyone. As far as Caitlyn goes, he refuses to help in any way. I did find out that he knows he isn't her father."

"Really? How did he find out?" Amanda asked.

"Well, it sounded like he tried to threaten his wife by saying he would take Caitlyn away from her if she tried to leave him. Her reaction to that threat was to tell him that he had no claim on Caitlyn—she wasn't his daughter."

"Did he believe her?" Amanda asked.

"No. But he had blood tests done, and they confirmed Catherine's story. He suspects that Andy is the father. But he doesn't seem to care in the least about Caitlyn, and I'm not sure he ever did."

"Is he at least going to report her missing?" Amanda asked. "When I checked with missing persons in Hamilton, they didn't have anything on her."

"No," Sarah responded. "He said he didn't care where she was and didn't want her back."

"Well, guess what," Amanda responded with obvious outrage. "He doesn't have that option. Our state approved Caylee's Law this year, and parents can be prosecuted for not reporting their missing child."

"Really? Is that named after that baby that went missing and was ultimately found dead?"

"Yes. The mother knew she was missing for a month and didn't report it. This law has gone into effect in five or six states and is being proposed in many others. We're one of the fortunate ones. It went into effect earlier this year!"

"That's great!" Sarah responded. "But will he still be responsible now that he knows he isn't the father?" Sarah asked.

"Yes! Absolutely! He's still the responsible caregiver."

"Well then, let's go tell him what he has to do," Sarah said enthusiastically.

"Slow down, my friend! Let the police handle this one." Amanda said emphatically. "I'll call Hamilton and let them know about the missing child. They'll follow up with Buckley and I'll let you know when it's done."

Several hours later, a female officer from Hamilton called Amanda and told her they were opening a missing child case on Caitlyn Buckley. She shared with Amanda that they'd gone to Buckley's house and offered him a ride to the police station to either file a missing person's report on his daughter or to be booked under Caylee's Law. His choice. Buckley grudgingly filed the report. Amanda thanked the officer and asked to be kept in the loop.

"Success!" Amanda announced cheerfully when she called Sarah later that day. "Now we have the Hamilton Police Department out there looking for Caitlyn!"

"Hooray!" Sarah cried.

Sarah called Sophie to catch her up on everything that had happened and to invite her to dinner. She had put lasagna in the oven right after Amanda called and hoped to celebrate the good news with Sophie. Sophie offered to bring a salad and the wine.

Sarah picked up the phone to call Charles and invite him as well, but hung up before dialing. She decided this celebration belonged to the two of them. Besides, she was hoping to talk Sophie into the hula hoop class and maybe, just maybe, after a couple of glasses of wine, Sophie would agree.

"*What?!*" Sophie screeched an hour later, sputtering wine across the table. "I'd be more likely to take a belly dancing class!"

"I was just hoping ..." Sarah began.

"Well, you can just keep hoping, kiddo. You aren't going to catch me making a fool of myself in some silly hula hoop class!"

"Okay. I'll drop the issue. And tomorrow I'll sign us both up for belly dancing," Sarah said nonchalantly.

"I'm not amused," Sophie responded with a frown as she helped herself to another slice of lasagna.

Sarah was not going to give up. "Well, no matter what you say, I see hooping in your future."

"Humph."

Chapter 13

It was a beautiful, warm day and Sarah wanted fresh air and sunshine. She called Charles and he agreed that it was a perfect day for a picnic. "Barney will love that," he said enthusiastically. "And, by the way, so will I," he added somewhat timidly. Things had been a bit strained between them since their confrontation after Sarah's trip to the Buckley home. He was pleased that she had suggested something fun and relaxing. They needed to spend that kind of time together.

"Where shall we go?" she asked when he arrived.

"Well, we can talk about that. I was thinking about suggesting that state park out toward Hamilton. I heard they have picnic sites and hiking trails. Are you up for a hike?" he asked.

"I'd love that!" she responded. She had missed several weeks of water aerobics and could feel the difference already. She was getting stiff and her flexibility was suffering. "It seems like, after a certain age, my joints seem to get rusty if I don't keep them moving."

"I know exactly what you mean," Charles responded. "After my physical therapy ended, I didn't keep up with the exercises, and I could feel how quickly I went downhill. The lap swimming really helps me."

Three years after Charles retired from the police department, he suffered a debilitating stroke which left him temporarily unable to speak or move his left side. After an extended hospitalization, he was moved to the nursing home in Cunningham Village for rehabilitation. By the time Sarah met him, he'd been discharged and was living in an independent apartment in the Village, but was still working with a physical therapist to build his strength. Swimming laps turned out to be his favorite exercise. Often he would swim laps at one end of the indoor pool while Sarah took her water aerobics class at the other end. He liked stealing glances at her walking past in her bathing suit.

Even in her late sixties, he found her to be a very striking woman. She had clearly maintained her weight and was conscientious about healthy eating and getting adequate exercise. She often talked to him about things she learned on the internet about living a healthy life style. He wasn't surprised when she joked about taking the hula hoop class. However, he adamantly refused to join her!

As they drove out of town, they talked about things going on at the center and classes they might take later in the year. Sarah told him about a design board she would like for him to help her make. He had no idea what a design board was, but he assured her that he would be happy to make it *with* her. He was careful not to say he would make it *for* her because he was beginning to understand that she was a very independent woman who wished to remain just that. His wife had been much more dependent on him. Of course, she had been ill for those last years. He enjoyed the feeling of being needed, but was learning to appreciate having a relationship with a woman who could hold her own.

When they arrived at the park, they decided to leave the lunches in the cooler and hike to the waterfall. They checked the map on the park's bulletin board and set off following the path up the hill. Barney pulled at his leash until he coughed, but there were signs saying dogs must be leashed. Charles spent a few minutes showing Barney how to do a modified heel and Barney picked it up immediately.

The three walked side by side with only a few exceptions, such as when a squirrel crossed their path and Barney took off so suddenly that the leash slipped right out of Sarah's hand. Fortunately, Barney stopped at the tree the squirrel had scampered up, and Charles was able to retrieve the leash while Barney was trying to follow the squirrel up the tree. As they walked away, Barney continued to stare at the squirrel on the outstretched limb with a puzzled look. *How did he do that?* Barney probably wondered.

All in all, it was a delightful day for all three. They took Barney's leash off for a few minutes and let him splash in the waterfall. Sarah took off her shoes and sat on the side of the stream with her feet dangling in the water. Charles secretly admired her dainty feet and slim ankles. Her hair had become curlier from the moisture and the exercise. He knew he was falling in love with this incredible woman and was so afraid of scaring her off. She seemed reluctant to move forward with their relationship. He wondered how she felt about him. Someday he would ask, but not today. Today was too perfect to take a chance.

At that moment, Barney came and stood close to them and shook. Water sprayed everywhere, and they both ducked, laughing. "Barney, stop!" Sarah cried but she was laughing too much for Barney to take her seriously. Once he felt sufficiently free of water, Barney moved close to her and gave her a kiss on the cheek. Charles reached over and kissed the opposite cheek. "Wow!" She declared. "How much loving can one woman take?"

You have no idea.

After their lunch, all three were relaxed and tired. Barney stretched out and took a nap while Charles and Sarah packed up. They headed home in the late afternoon. Charles walked them to their door and kissed Sarah gently. She smiled at him and her eyes glistened. *Is that love I see in her eyes,* he wondered.

* * * * *

The telephone rang just as Sarah got into bed. She reached over to answer it but couldn't see the caller ID from her angle. "Andy!" she squealed enthusiastically when she heard his voice. "I was hoping you would call today."

"I'm sorry I took so long getting back to you, Sarah. I didn't want to call at all. I've caused you enough trouble already."

"Andy. Stop. We need to talk right away."

"You know where Caitlyn is?" Andy asked hopefully.

"No, Andy. But we have a plan. How and where can we get together? It's too involved to go into on the phone."

Andy was silent for a minute. Then he spoke and said, "Is there any way you can come to Hamilton? I hate to ask that of you, but ..."

"Yes! I'll come and I need to bring Sophie and Charles with me...."

"But …" he interrupted.

"Yes, Andy. They need to come. They're part of the plan. You won't be disappointed."

"Okay. You can all come to my room. I'll change hotels after that so you can honestly say you don't know where I am if you're questioned."

"That may not be necessary, Andy. I'll explain when we get together. Okay, where and when?"

"I'm in Hamilton at the Sheffield. It's an old rundown hotel on the east side. I was sure I'd see Caitlyn over here. For all I know I have," he said regretfully. "I probably wouldn't know her if I sat next to her in the soup kitchen. Oh, speaking of eating at the soup kitchen … what did you find in the quilt?"

"We need to talk about that, too, when we get together. Not now … and what does that have to do with eating in the soup kitchen?" Sarah asked.

"I'm running out of money and I was just hoping … but then … there's probably nothing in the quilt. Anyway, we'll talk about it when you get here. When can you come?"

"Tomorrow?"

"That's good." They discussed a time and Andy gave her directions. He warned her to park close to the hotel and be extremely careful. It was a dangerous part of town. "Be sure you aren't followed," he added.

Sarah hoped the others would be available. She didn't have any way to reach Andy to make changes. After they hung up, Sarah peeked out the window and saw that Sophie's lights were still on. She pulled her trench coat on over her gown and hurried across the street.

"Hi'ya, Gal," Sophie greeted as she opened the door. "You look excited. What's happening?"

"I heard from Andy, and I'm sure hoping you're available tomorrow. He agreed to meet us at his room in Hamilton. Are you game?"

"I'm in," Sophie announced.

"Okay, then we'll see if Charles is available."

"Charles?" Sophie asked, looking surprised. "Charles can't meet with Andy. Remember, he said he would be obligated to turn him in even though he's retired."

"Nonsense." Sarah retorted. "He's taking his oath way too seriously."

"Well, he's your honey bunny," Sophie said dismissively, then added, "but I know what I heard when we talked about this."

"Hmm. I think you might be right. But now I'm between a rock and a hard place. Charles doesn't want me placing myself in danger, but he doesn't want to be there with me."

"So," Sophie concluded, "that means it's up to you to decide. Will it be *rock* or *hard place*?"

"You're right. Let's go."

"What's so dangerous about this mission anyway?" Sophie asked. "Andy's certainly no danger."

"No, not from Andy. It's just a very rough part of town. At first, Andy didn't want Charles there. Then he said he was glad we'd have him with us for protection."

"Humph. When did we ever need protection? Wasn't that you and me out at that hobo camp last year?" Sophie said, snickering proudly. "We can take care of ourselves, kiddo. Besides, I have mace."

"He said for us to make sure we aren't followed," Sarah said with a mischievous smile.

"How cloak and dagger is that!" Sophie responded. "This could be fun."

They sat down at the kitchen table and planned their strategy. "I hope Andy will go for this. It's the only chance he stands of getting out of prison before his daughter is a grandmother," Sophie predicted.

Chapter 14

Sophie and Sarah decided to take Sophie's Jeep. "It looks tough," Sophie said. "We can't arrive in that sissy car of yours. We'll be laughed out of town."

Sarah had wanted to drive. Sophie was easily distracted by her own story telling and sometimes appeared to have forgotten she was behind the wheel. "Okay, Sophie. You drive but no stories today."

"Humph."

After they left the Village and turned onto the dual highway to Hamilton for the second time that week, Sophie turned to Sarah and said, "Did you hear about Virginia at the Saturday night social?" Not waiting for an answer, Sophie dived into an hilarious account of Virginia and her husband doing the twist. Both of the Warrens were in their late eighties and both needed assistance with walking. Fred used a walker and Virginia had a cane. The description of the two of them doing the twist with their assistive devices banging into each other was hilarious, and both women laughed until tears ran down their cheeks. Suddenly, Sarah realized Sophie was not watching where she was going and was headed up the wrong side of the road.

Fortunately, no one was coming the other way when Sarah screamed, "Sophie, watch where you're going!" Sophie jerked the wheel to the right and straightened the Jeep up in the proper lane.

"Sorry," she said wiping tears from her cheeks as she tried to hold back the laughter. "But it *was* funny," she added with one more chuckle.

"That's it," Sarah said, looking serious. "No more stories."

They drove in silence for another few miles when Sophie said, "Did you hear about … ?"

"Quiet," Sarah demanded.

"Humph."

The rest of the drive was uneventful. Sarah told Sophie about her quilt class and the Underground Railroad and how blocks might have been used. Sophie listened, looking just a bit bored, but Sarah continued because it kept Sophie's eyes on the road. "I'll show them to you when we get home," Sarah added. "I think that's our turnoff right up there. ..."

Sophie took the turnoff and Sarah read the directions Andy had given her. Charles had programmed the GPS, but she was more comfortable with her hand-written directions. She would turn the GPS on if they got lost.

"Did he program that thing to get me back home?" Sophie asked.

"You just hit *go home*."

"How does it know where I live?" Sophie asked suspiciously.

"It will bring you to my house. I think you know the way from there. If not, I'll give you *written directions*," Sarah teased. "Turn right at the next light."

Sophie made the turn. After several more turns, Sarah said, "Slow down. I think it's in this block." Straight ahead they saw a tattered awning with the letters *SH-F--ELD*. "That's it. Over there on the left. Park wherever you can," Sarah added. There were several people on the sidewalk outside the hotel. The women were scantily dressed for such a cool day. The men appeared to be in some sort of negotiation.

"Buying drugs," Sophie said, with authority.

"How do you know that?" Sarah asked.

"Well, it's obvious. The one with all those tattoos is the dealer. The other two guys are looking for their next score," Sophie explained.

"You watch too much television."

Sophie parked the car and the two women locked up and headed for the Sheffield. As they approached the entrance, the woman in red shorts and a sparkly halter said, "Hey girls, this is our spot."

Everyone standing around howled with laughter. One of the men called over and said, "They're kinda cute. I think I'll bring my grandpa next time!" Sophie and Sarah ignored the hoots and hollers that followed and entered the building.

Andy had told them to come up the back stairs, and he was in room 305. Sophie got to the second floor without complaining but refused to go any farther. "That's an elevator over there," she said pointing to a metal door with an up and down arrow painted on it.

"Andy said not to use it. It gets stuck. I don't want to spend the day, or possibly the week, waiting for someone to get us out. Come on. One more floor."

Sophie sighed and began to slowly climb the last flight with Sarah behind her. "Now," Sarah said laughing, "I feel obligated to point out to you that you wouldn't be having all this trouble climbing the stairs if you took the hula hoop class and got into shape." Sophie tried to respond but was too winded to talk.

Once they got to the third floor and Sophie caught her breath, she said, "Don't think you can trick me into taking that confounded class of yours!"

"There's his room," Sarah said, ignoring Sophie and pointing up the dark hallway. "Poor Andy. He doesn't belong in a place like this." She walked up to the door and tapped lightly. "Andy, it's us."

Andy opened the door and, with tears in his eyes, hugged both women. The room was small and contained a dilapidated-looking bed, a wooden chair, and a floor lamp. There was a box on the floor which contained a few items of clothing. He told them the bathroom was up the hall if they needed it. They both declined. "I'd offer to get you something, but, as you can see, there's nothing to get. We could go across the street for coffee, but I can't guarantee they wash the cups." Sarah, looking around at how Andy was living, suspected he just might be glad to get back to Evanston.

"Take the chair, Sophie," Sarah offered. "I'll sit on the bed." Sophie looked at the chair suspiciously and said that she would prefer the bed, too. Andy pulled the chair over facing the bed and sat down facing them.

"Okay, girls. What's this all about?"

Sarah began and, again, Sophie interjected where she saw fit. Together they explained their plan. They told him that Amanda had assured them that the only way to avoid an extensive prison sentence would be for him to turn himself in voluntarily.

"Amanda?" Andy looked worried. "Isn't Amanda your cop friend?"

"Yes. But she's helping us. She said to tell you that it's no guarantee, but that the judge is likely to be more lenient if you turn yourself in. She also said the judge would probably be willing to take into consideration your reason for leaving."

"That's taking a big chance," Andy said reluctantly. "It'll all depend on the judge?"

"That's right," Sophie said. "But if the police pick you up you stand no chance at all of a reduced sentence. It's like I told Sarah, you would be lucky to get out before your daughter is a grandmother!"

"Let me get this straight," Andy said frowning at the two women sitting on his bed. "Your plan is for me to go back and, hopefully, have a less severe sentence. How does that help me? I don't care about the sentence. I want to find my daughter."

"That's the best part of the plan, Andy," Sarah began. "Once you're safely back in prison, Charles has agreed to help us find Caitlyn. The three of us will find her. And, besides that, Amanda was able to get Buck to report her to Missing Persons. The entire Hamilton Police Department is out there searching for her!"

"We just don't want them to find *you* in the process!" Sophie added.

Andy looked overwhelmed. He rested his elbows on his knees and held his head in his hands. When he finally looked up, Sarah could see tears standing in his eyes. She couldn't read his reaction to what they'd said. She and Sophie waited for him to speak.

Finally, he wiped his eyes on the tail of his shirt. Sarah could see his ribs as he lifted his shirt and knew he had lost a great deal of weight. He had been on the street well over a month and probably had very little to eat. "I'll do it," Andy said softly. "I'll do it if you promise to find her *and* take care of her until I get out."

"We'll do both, Andy. We'll need to take this one step at a time, but I think, once we find her, we need to establish paternity. That will get her out of the clutches of that Buck character." Sarah continued, "Then we need to get a temporary guardian and I'd be more than happy to be that person."

The tears Andy had been struggling to control flowed down his cheeks. "You mean it, Sarah?"

"Of course, I mean it. What do you say? Is it a deal?"

"It's a deal," he said, smiling through his tears.

"Let's call Amanda now." Andy stood and put his few scattered belongings into the box while Sarah pulled her cell phone out of her bag.

"Amanda. I'm with Andy. He's coming in. Can you meet us?"

Amanda said that Sarah should drive him to the Middletown police station but that she and Sophie should remain outside. "Andy should walk in alone and head straight for the desk sergeant," she continued. "He should immediately say who he is and that he's there to turn himself in. That's what will look best for him."

"Okay. I'll explain that to him. Will you be able to see him at all?"

"I want you to call me on my cell when you arrive outside the station. I'll walk out to the sergeant's desk and offer to take over. That way, I can walk him, personally, through the process," Amanda explained.

"How can we ever thank you, Amanda," Sarah said affectionately.

"You can bake me one of those double chocolate cakes like you made for Charles' birthday," she responded and both women laughed.

"Call me tonight, if you can, and let me know how it goes," Sarah requested.

"I'll do it. Good work, Detective Sarah Miller," Amanda said with a chuckle.

The three left Andy's room and walked down the dark, dingy hall, Andy holding his box and the two women looking very out of place. Sophie stopped at the top of the stairs and gave Sarah a pleading look.

"It's easier going downhill," Sarah teased, smiling at Sophie.

Chapter 15

Sarah woke up feeling relaxed and fresh after a long and peaceful night's sleep. Barney greeted her with a smile and the two went into the kitchen, Barney to the backyard and Sarah to the coffee pot. Sarah smiled when she saw the coffee, brewed and ready to pour. Charles had given her a new electric pot which had the coffee ready when she got up in the mornings. The smell wafted through the house, waking her up with its delicious aroma every day.

Once she poured her coffee, let Barney back in, and sat down at the table, she found herself still smiling. Amanda had called the night before with encouraging news about Andy. Andy's attorney met with the district attorney and asked that he recommend the new charges be dismissed. He argued this based on the fact that Andy had turned himself in, and there was no violence involved in his escape. He simply walked away. His lawyer and the district attorney came to an agreement, and they will make the recommendation to the court.

Amanda said she thinks there's a good chance the court will agree. Andy has friends among the guards who'll probably testify for him. He'll also have an opportunity to tell the judge why he felt he had to leave. Depending on the judge, Andy may simply return to prison and continue serving his original sentence. The judge might add time, but Amanda didn't think he would. She said the worst case might be that Andy wouldn't be paroled as soon as he had expected. The attorney agreed that it may go against him at his next parole hearing.

Andy was going to be okay. He might not get out as soon as he had hoped, but he was going to be okay. With the Hamilton Police Department looking for Caitlyn, Sarah felt hopeful and didn't feel the pressure to be out there trying to find her alone.

Amanda had talked with a friend of hers on the Hamilton force who agreed to keep Amanda informed of their progress. Hamilton had already filed all the reports that are required when children are missing or abducted, including notifying the FBI. They began their investigation and were interviewing staff and students at her school, and, of course, doing extensive questioning of Buckley and his neighbors.

"Life is good," Sarah said aloud, quoting one of her favorite tee-shirts.

Sarah looked at the clock and realized she was going to be late for class if she didn't get moving. She put a piece of cheese on a slice of bread, folded it over, and took off for the sewing room to pack her quilter's tote. She would see if Charles wanted to come over in the afternoon and hang the design board she had made using the foam board and cotton batting.

* * * * *

Katie explained that she would be filling in for Ruth today and pointed to the Flying Geese block in the sampler quilt hanging in the classroom. "This is today's block. It's called Flying Geese and its message in the springtime was probably something like 'follow the geese as they fly north.' We won't be doing the North Star block, but that's another one that seems to point the way north."

"Here are your instructions," Katie said, passing out the sheets Ruth had left for her. "Read them through and see what you can do on your own. Come get me if you have any problems. I see two customers in the front. I'll be right back."

Delores spoke up saying, "I'm very familiar with this block and can answer questions until you get back if you'd like."

"Great!" Katie responded with a smile. Delores was a seasoned quilter; Katie knew the class would be in good hands if the customers took more time than she expected.

Everyone studied their sheets and started working on their blocks, except Dottie. "What're we supposed to do?" Dottie asked without picking up the instruction sheet. Delores patiently moved to the chair next to her and walked her through the steps. She then walked around and watched what the others were doing. Katie had come back into the room and stepped back to watch. Delores stopped by Kimberly and gently helped her to rearrange her fabric on the cutting board to make it easier to cut. Katie knew her mother wanted to hire a teacher for several hours a week. *Delores might be just the ticket.*

After class, Sarah purchased a book which contained the story of the Underground Railroad and had examples of all the blocks that were reportedly used as secret messages. She had decided to begin making extra blocks at home so she could enlarge the quilt to a queen size for Charles. She would need to ask Ruth to help her with the calculations.

Sarah hurried home, eager to call Charles and see if he was available to come hang the design board. He hadn't seen the blocks she was working on, but she might put them on the board and see his reaction. He, of course, wouldn't know they were for him. She felt sure he would like them once she told him some of the stories. He was somewhat of a history buff. She also wanted to let him know that Andy was securely back in prison. She hoped he would have some ideas about what they could do to help find Caitlyn.

*   *   *   *   *

The young girl sat on the bench in the Hamilton bus station with her knees pulled up to her chin. She wore jeans and a pink tee-shirt with words printed on the front. The way she was sitting, the words weren't visible.

She wasn't crying, but her eyes were red and swollen. The man watching her thought she had been crying. Her hair was disheveled and her clothes soiled. She looked straight ahead, not acknowledging the presence of the people around her.

After a while, the man moved and sat beside her. He spoke to her gently. "Are you okay, young lady?" She didn't answer.

He waited awhile and again attempted to speak with her. "I've been watching you and wondering if you're lost or alone. Do you need help?"

The girl was young, but not naive. She didn't trust the man. She didn't trust most men. She straightened up, picked up her duffle bag, and walked across the noisy room. She entered the ladies room, sat down on a wooden chair someone had placed near the door and waited for the man to leave. Her bus wasn't due for several hours. She would stay here for a while.

She had a few dollars, maybe forty after paying for the ticket. That would last her for a few days if she could find a shelter. She wasn't sure if the police were looking for her, but she thought it was unlikely.

She didn't run away; her father threw her out. Or actually the man she used to think was her father. Now he said he isn't her father. It made sense to her. He never acted like a father and she never loved him.

Wouldn't you just naturally love your father? she wondered.

The girl worried about getting picked up by the police even if the man who was no longer her father didn't report her missing. She was fourteen, almost fifteen, but she had a small, undeveloped build and looked much younger.

She didn't want to get turned over to social services. Several kids in her school lived in foster homes and they hated it. *But then, it might not be too bad. I'd have a place to live and food, and I could go to school.*

She really hadn't thought it through when she left. He said, "Pack and get out," so she did. As far as she knew, there weren't any relatives except some woman in Middletown. Her mother took her there a few times. The girl didn't know who she was; her mother called her aunt something. *I guess that would make her my great aunt.*

She and her mother were never close. Her mother was *sick* most mornings, sleeping in until afternoon. The young girl got herself to school every day and got good grades, although no one ever asked to see them. She missed her mother anyway.

A tear slipped down her cheek and she wiped it away almost violently. "No crying!" She told herself aloud. No one was in the room to hear her.

Chapter 16

"**I**'m here," Charles called from the front porch. As he stood at the screen door, he felt the soft warm breeze on his bare arms. *I'm actually happy. At this moment, standing on this spot, I'm totally happy.* It had been many years since Charles was able to feel happiness. After his retirement and his wife's death, followed by his stroke and many months of recuperation, he had lost the feeling of joy. He smiled, and again called through the screen door, "I'm here, Sarah."

"Come on back," Sarah called. "I'm in the sewing room."

Charles wiped his feet on the mat outside the screen door and again on the rug at the entryway. Sarah kept a very clean and orderly home. The cushions on her couch and matching chair were upholstered in a soft brown. She had a beautiful flowery quilt over the back of the couch and a matching pillow on the chair.

Her furniture, which he had thought was Mission style, was actually Arts and Crafts from the turn of the century, as Sarah had explained. Although it looked new to him, she said it had belonged to her grandmother who grew up in Kentucky. The wood was stained a warm, soft brown, almost the color of the cushions. The only contrast came from the rose carpet and the colorful floral quilt. It was a warm, comfortable room. Sarah had fresh flowers on the coffee table along with a pile of quilt books and magazines.

He walked straight through the kitchen and eating area toward the sewing room at the back of the house. On his way past Sarah's room, he stopped to look. The colors were soft greens and browns with a touch of rose. He noticed there was no quilt on her bed. He was surprised she hadn't made one yet.

"What's taking you so long?" Sarah called cheerfully from the sewing room. "It's only about twenty steps from the front door to the sewing room." She laughed as he entered the room looking embarrassed.

"Just sightseeing," he explained. "Your home is so warm and cozy."

"That's what a home should be," she responded with a smile. She presented her cheek for a kiss, but he reached beyond her cheek and gave her a soft kiss on the lips. She smiled again and gave him a mischievous look. He wondered what that look meant, but knew he would never figure out women and their many expressions. He just smiled back and shrugged.

"So. Where's my project?" Charles asked.

She pulled out a large piece of foam board with cotton batting neatly attached to it. There was about one inch which wrapped around to the back.

"How did you get this attached so smoothly?"

"The miracle of spray adhesive," Sarah responded, "and yes, I did it in the backyard so I wouldn't breathe the fumes," she added, anticipating his objection.

"How did you know I was going to say that?" *How is it that she can anticipate what I'm going to say before I even think it? I'm not sure what she is saying even after she says it? Women are a mystery!* Charles had been married for forty years to the same woman, his high school sweetheart. He hadn't dated since she died. He didn't like to think of himself as naive, but that's exactly what he was.

They found a place to hang the design board so that Sarah could place blocks on it and back away from it to get the full effect. "So let me show you some blocks," Sarah said excitedly after the board was safely hung. She grabbed her quilter's tote and carefully removed her six blocks. She lined them up on the design board leaving an inch or so between each one. "When they go into the quilt," Sarah explained, "there will be fabric between each one, probably a one- or two-inch strip to separate them.

"I love these," Charles said, examining them closely. "The fabric looks old, like you see in antique quilts in the museum."

"These fabrics are reproductions of fabrics used in the 1800s," Sarah explained. She went on to tell Charles about the possible use of quilts during the Civil War, and, pulling one block off the board at a time, she told the related stories that Ruth had told the class."

"This is fascinating!" Charles exclaimed. "Are there other blocks?"

"Yes, come look at this book." She grabbed her new *Quilts from the 1800s* book and, together, they moved into the kitchen. She pulled a pitcher of lemonade out of the fridge and grabbed a few cookies from the cookie jar. Barney, of course, stood by his own cookie jar looking pitiful, so she grabbed a few for him too. Barney took his treats to his corner while Sarah joined Charles at the table. They spent the next hour going through the book, both enjoying the artistry and the history. Sarah was pleased to see how interested he was in the stories and the blocks. *He will love his quilt!*

"Are you making this for your bed?" Charles asked.

"This one is definitely a bed quilt," she answered vaguely, hoping he didn't pursue the subject.

"Let's take Barney for a walk," he said suddenly. "Just look out there at your garden! I'll bet the park is beautiful right now."

"Great idea," she responded, glad that the topic was changed. "How about a walk, Barney?" He jumped up, ran in circles around them, finally grabbing his leash from the hook and bringing it to her. As she reached for it, he backed away and stood in front of Charles instead. "Well, I guess I've been replaced," she said, teasing the two of them.

As they walked, Sarah asked Charles if he had any ideas about looking for Caitlyn.

"I've been thinking," Charles responded, "that I might drive over to Hamilton and talk to the Department. I have some friends over there who haven't retired yet. Maybe I could offer to help out with this case."

"Oh, Charles," Sarah exclaimed with her hands on her cheeks in astonishment. "That would be wonderful. With all your experience and your personal interest in the case, you'd be a great help to them."

"Well, sometimes being personally involved isn't always a good thing, but I might be able to offer some needed legwork," he responded.

By this time, they were more than half-way to town and Charles suggested they get ice cream. "Good idea," Sarah said, enthusiastically. "Let's go to Persnickety. Bea's ice cream is delicious and I'd love to see her." As they approached the shop, a young girl was walking away from the gazebo carrying a duffle bag.

"I don't know who she is," Bea said as she scooped their ice cream. "She sat out there for an hour or so yesterday. I went out and asked her if she would like ice cream, but she said no and left. I was surprised to see her there when I opened the shop this morning, but I decided not to intrude."

"She looked so young and fragile. I wonder where she belongs," Sarah said thoughtfully, then dug into her ice cream with gusto.

Chapter 17

As Ruth drove toward Ohio and to the home she had walked away from so many years before, she thought how angry her father had been and how hurt her mother was when she brought Nathan home to meet them. Nathan was born in Pennsylvania and lived among the Amish there and was well aware of what marrying Ruth would mean. He was not Amish.

Ruth met Nathan in art school. Although Ruth was an excellent quilter, the art school in Columbus was offering a special program in fabric art. Ruth had seen a poster advertising the program which showed quilts that were so beautiful, they brought tears to her eyes. "They touched my heart, Mama," she had said pleadingly. "I want to go learn."

Her father had been adamantly opposed to the idea. "You have chores right here," he grumbled. Her mother understood how she felt; she, too, was a creative quilter. After many family discussions, her father reluctantly agreed to allow her to travel to Columbus for one term. He made it very clear he was not pleased about this and refused to pay for any of it. Ruth used the money she had been saving from her vegetable stand and was able to get a small scholarship.

As it turned out, Ruth returned home six months later married to an English boy. Her father believed in a strict interpretation of Amish tradition and refused to accept the marriage. He had turned them out of the house and told Ruth she was no longer family.

It was late afternoon when Ruth turned off the Interstate. She thought about the phone call from her brother, Jacob, telling her about their father's illness. He said it was very serious. She loved her father and hoped to see him, if only to say goodbye. She had never been angry with him; she understood the Amish way. It had been her life for seventeen years.

Driving down the dirt road, Ruth could see the house in the distance. It looked freshly painted. Behind the house stood the silo and the barns. She didn't remember the second barn. She hadn't been home for more than twenty years. *Things change.*

Ruth turned slowing into the rutted path beside the house. Looking past the house, she could see her mother's Bow Tie quilt hanging on the line, gently swaying in time with the light breeze. *How many nights I have slept under that quilt! I must not cry.* For a moment, she wished Katie were with her.

Her hand was trembling as she knocked on the screen door. The front door was open and the familiar smell of stew wafted toward her. She fought the tears that were gathering behind her eyes. "Mama," she muttered, too softly for anyone to hear.

A handsome young man came to the door. "Hello," he greeted with a smile. When Ruth didn't respond, he added kindly, "Can we help you?"

"I'm Ruth," was all she could say without crying.

"Ruth," the young man said excitedly. "Ruth!" He opened the screen door and threw his arms around her. "I'm Jacob. I'm so glad you came."

"Jacob?" Ruth repeated joyfully. He was only six years old when she left. Her mother had seven children and Ruth had taken on most of the responsibility for Jacob and for the youngest girl, Anna. She and Jacob hugged and allowed their tears to flow.

"How old are you now?" Ruth asked. "About twenty-five?"

"Twenty-eight exactly," he said proudly. "Yesterday was my birthday. I live here with my wife, Rebecca. We've taken care of Mama since her stroke."

Her stroke? Ruth had no idea her mother had been ill. She'd missed so much.

"How is Papa?" Ruth asked tentatively. "Is he here?"

"No. He's in the hospital. We got him there, fighting the whole way, and now he's fighting to get back home. I think he'll come back tomorrow." He dropped his eyes and added sadly, "He knows he's dying and he wants to die at home." After a pause, he added, "It'll be hard on Mama for him to be here, but it's probably for the best."

"And Mama … how is she?"

"Since her stroke, she hasn't been herself. She can't get around and her memory is bad. Rebecca is wonderful with her and has taken over all the chores. You'll love Rebecca. She has been a Godsend."

"I wish I'd known about Mama's stroke," Ruth said, wondering why they called her now, but not then.

"We tried," Jacob said. "Papa wouldn't allow it. I'm sorry."

"I understand," she responded warmly. "Do you think Mama will see me today?"

"Papa wouldn't want you to come into the house and Mama would never go against him. But I think she can make it to the porch, if she will. I'll go ask." He gave her one last hug and hurried into the house.

Ruth sat in the wicker chair and waited. Finally Jacob returned with her mother, looking old and frail, hanging onto his arm for support. Tears ran down her cheeks when she saw Ruth. Ruth immediately got up and Jacob guided their mother to the chair. Ruth fell to her knees in front of her mother and they held each other's hands. Both wept.

"I love you, Mama," she said softly.

Her mother nodded and smiled through her tears.

Rebecca came out to meet Ruth and offered to bring coffee and pastries out on the porch. Jacob brought three more chairs from the kitchen. The four sat outside for several hours, weeping at first, then talking and ultimately laughing as they recalled their shared past.

Then, in a more serious tone, Ruth asked, "Is there any way I can see Papa?"

"No, honey," her mother responded, but using the German dialect spoken by the Amish. "You know we can't do that. We won't go against his wishes, especially now. I'm sorry."

"I understand," Ruth said, following her mother's lead and using her childhood language. She squeezed her mother's hand and said, "Mama, I want you to know that I'm very happy. We're all three happy. We own a quilt shop in Middletown and have many friends. Katie works with me;

in fact, today she's teaching a class on how to make the Flying Geese quilt block."

Her mother laughed. "I remember teaching you how to make that block when you were seven years old. You were a good quilter even then. And you started basting my quilts when you were only five! Your running stitch was perfect!"

"My running stitch?" Ruth laughed. "That's what I named my shop! Running Stitches." Her mother, who'd come outside looking so old and frail, was now bright and gleaming as she laughed. *Oh, how I miss my family.*

The four continued to talk until dusk. Abruptly, her mother asked, "How is little Katie? Can she walk yet?" Ruth was puzzled by the question, but Jacob tapped her on the shoulder and shook his head. Suddenly, she realized her mother had become confused. Later, as she was getting into her car, Jacob would explain that she gets worse at night. "The doctor called it 'Sundowners,'" he said. "Sometimes she doesn't even know Rebecca and me."

Finally, Ruth answered her mother's question by saying, "Katie is one of the reasons I came, Mama. She wants to know her family."

Her mother looked sad but the confusion seemed to have passed. "You know we can't do that, Ruth. Not while Papa is alive."

"I know," Ruth said sadly. "I know." The obvious remained unspoken.

Her mother hesitated, as if she were deciding whether or not to speak. Finally, she took a deep breath and very coherently said, "Your sister Anna has left the Amish way. She married a young English boy she met during her *rumspringa*. She lives in …" she hesitated, but then added confidently, "… Williams County. She lives in Williams County, not far from here, with the boy's family. We don't see her anymore, of course, but you could." She searched Ruth's eyes and added, "I think that would be good for both of you."

Ruth got directions to Anna's house and, after a few more minutes of visiting, the four hugged, wept, and parted. Jacob promised to keep Ruth informed about their father's illness. As Ruth was driving away, she could see that it took Jacob and Rebecca both to get the frail woman back into the house.

Ruth was emotionally and physically exhausted as she drove. She thought she would spend the night outside of town and visit her sister the next day, but once she got settled into the motel room and called Nathan, she decided to head back home the next morning. She would plan a visit after she talked to Anna and, hopefully, bring Katie along.

Chapter 18

Sarah arrived at the shop an hour before her class time. She wanted to make a quilt for her own bed but still hadn't decided on a pattern. She wasn't ready to start it yet, but was eager to have a plan and maybe even the fabrics. When Ruth came out of the stock room, Sarah smiled and asked, "How was your trip?"

"It went better than I expected," Ruth responded. "Papa was still in the hospital and Mama was willing to come out on the porch. We visited for several hours out there." Ruth was beaming, and Sarah knew how happy she must be to have made a connection with her family. Ruth went on to tell Sarah about the visit and, in particular, about her sister Anna. "We will visit Anna soon," Ruth said confidently.

"Both of you?"

"Yes! That's what so good about it. Finally Katie can meet a few relatives and, in time, perhaps more. I know she yearns for that connection." Ruth was rearranging the patterns and the two women began talking about Sarah's quilt and, ultimately, pulled out several bolts of fabric which Sarah thought she would like in her bedroom.

"I'm not ready to make the quilt," Sarah said hesitantly, "but I love this fabric. What if it's gone when I'm ready to make the quilt?"

Ruth simply smiled knowingly. How often she had heard that very statement! "Well, Sarah, some people buy two or three yards of what they truly love even if they don't know for sure how they'll use it."

"This goes with it perfectly, don't you think?" Sarah asked, holding up a second bolt.

"Yes! That's a beautiful combination."

A half hour later, Sarah was laying her credit card on the counter while Ruth put the four fabrics of varying lengths into a bag. Sarah had included three yards of her favorite one, assuming she would want that for the border and for some of the blocks. The rest coordinated beautifully. She had no idea what pattern she would use, but when Ruth spread the fabrics out on the cutting table, the combination made her feel calm and peaceful. There was no doubt that these were the fabrics Sarah wanted in her bedroom.

The other members of the sampler class began to arrive. Sarah put her bag of fabrics under her table and greeted the students as they came in. Delores and Danny were the first to arrive. Christina and Kimberly came in next and sat down at a shared table. "Say, Sarah," Kimberly began. "You were interested in seeing our Sears Roebuck house sometime and we just had a long-arm quilting machine delivered. We had them set it up in the bedroom Papa added for his mother on the back of the house. We aren't very good at quilting on it yet, but we were wondering if you would like to come see it."

"Oh, Kimberly, I'd love that. I've never seen a long-arm. I'm going to be finishing a quilt soon. Are you planning to take in quilts for machine quilting or is this just for yourselves?" Sarah asked eagerly.

"If you saw the price tag on this machine, you wouldn't be asking. I figure we're going to have to do one quilt every hour, 24-7, in order to pay for this machine in our lifetime!" Everyone was listening at this point and they all laughed.

"Well, you'll get plenty of business from this shop," Ruth said as she entered the room. "Just print up some cards and put them on the checkout counter where everyone will see them. I can almost guarantee you'll be busy 24-7."

Ruth put a new block on the design board and said, "This is our seventh block and it's called Jacob's Ladder. Many of the safe houses had false walls which concealed ladders down to an underground space. This block may have referred to those special hiding places."

As she explained the block and passed out the instructions, Dottie came rushing in carrying her six-year-old under her arm. "Sorry I'm late. Samantha has a temperature and I couldn't send her to school." Dottie placed the child in the chair next to her own and immediately, she laid her head down on the table. Sarah noticed that the girl was trembling.

"I think she's having a chill, Dottie. She should be home in bed or at the doctor. Not here."

"But I can't miss the class. I've already paid for it and I have my material."

Ruth intervened, saying, "Dottie, Sarah is right. I'll help you catch up with the class, but your child is very sick. Please take her to the doctor." Dottie huffed and gathered up her child and her tote bag and headed for the door. She was muttering, but the group couldn't hear what she was saying.

Katie stuck her head in the classroom and asked, "What was that all about? Did you actually throw Dottie out?"

"Of course not, Katie. What made you think that?" Ruth responded.

"She was mumbling that she has been 'thrown out of better places than this' as she went out the door." The group snickered and went back to work on their blocks.

Sarah finished early and quietly excused herself and gathered up her materials and her bags of new fabric. Sarah was feeling good and wanted to share her happiness with Barney. There was a pet shop a few doors up the street from Stitches, so she put her bags in the car and walked to Paws & Claws.

Once inside, she perused the shelves of treats and dog toys, undecided between the two. Barney loved treats but the vet said he had put on a little weight so she decided on a toy. Since he needed exercise, she found a ball attached to a heavy rope. The picture on the tag showed a boy throwing the ball and the dog leaping into the air to catch it by the rope. She could see Charles and Barney having a grand time with it.

As she was getting ready to pay for the toy, she grabbed a box of treats as well. "He deserves both," she told the youngster who was ringing her up.

Driving home, she thought about putting her newly acquired fabric into the oak cabinet in her sewing room. But thinking of the cabinet caused her smile to fade. *The quilt. I must do something about the missing quilt.* She still hadn't reported it missing. By the time she pulled into her driveway, she had decided to call Amanda after lunch and tell her about it. She wasn't ready to tell Andy it was missing, but she needed to report it to the police. Obviously, someone

had been in her house. It took her many weeks to be willing
to acknowledge that simple fact.

Of course, the faded smile immediately returned as
Barney met her at the door. He was always ecstatic when
she returned, whether she had been gone five hours or five
minutes.

Barney had been picked up behind Barney's Bar & Grill
and the staff at the Humane Society had named him Barney
by default. But the name fit him perfectly. Even though he
wasn't much to look at when Sarah brought him home, after
a few trips to the Puppy Parlor, even Sophie had to admit he
looked almost handsome.

Mostly it was Barney's personality that won over anyone
who came into his world. When meeting strangers, he was
somewhat reticent at first, but always gave them a chance.
Ultimately, he loved almost everyone he came in contact
with, but he worshiped Sarah. It was as if he realized she had
saved him from an uncertain future and provided him with
a life filled with love. He was a very happy dog.

Sarah took the rope-ball toy out of the bag, sat down on
the couch, and placed the toy on her lap. He came over and
sniffed it. Then he looked deep into Sarah's eyes. "Yes," she
said. "It's yours!" She tossed it across the room and he ran
to get it.

He picked it up by the rope and immediately returned it
to her lap. He sat at her feet with his tail rapidly swinging
back and forth. He made a slight noise in his throat, not
quite a bark. Sarah tossed it again, and again he returned it.
"Let's go out in the backyard and play," Sarah said, and the
two hurried to the backdoor and spent the next hour playing
in the warm sunshine.

When they came in, Sarah again thought about the quilt and Amanda. "I can't keep putting this off," she told herself, and picked up the phone.

"Sarah. I'm glad you called," Amanda said right away when she answered the phone. "I want to talk with you, too."

"Has something happened?" Sarah asked apprehensively.

"No, no. I'm sorry to alarm you. Nothing has happened. I just wanted to find out how you're doing and to let you know what has been going on with Andy."

"Well, I have something to talk with you about, Amanda. Is there any chance you can come over?"

"Of course. I have a report to finish and then I'm off. Can I come by on my way home?"

"Sure. How about having a light supper with me?" Sarah was planning to make a dinner salad and quickly figured that she could defrost a couple of chicken breasts to put on top.

"I'd love that," Amanda replied. "I'll be there around six, okay?"

"Good. See you then." Sarah quickly removed the chicken breasts and put them in the microwave to defrost. She then cut the vegetables and put them in the refrigerator, so she wouldn't have much to do when Amanda got there. She put a bottle of Chardonnay in to cool and removed a package of crescent rolls ready to bake along with the chicken. "It's not exactly a celebration," she said to Barney, "but it will be nice to spend some time with Amanda." Barney smiled and dragged his new toy into his corner of the kitchen.

When Amanda arrived, Sarah suggested they have a glass of wine and sit down to their salads before getting into their various issues. She knew she was putting off the inevitable, but another hour or so wouldn't matter.

"You haven't been to the Friday night quilt group yet," Sarah said curiously. "Have you changed your mind?"

"Absolutely not!" Amanda responded emphatically. "It's just that I have three new cases, all needing my attention. I hardly have time to grab a few hours of sleep." She took a sip of her wine and asked Sarah what the Friday night group has been doing. They talked about the group and quilts in general and Sarah's projects in particular. After eating, Sarah brought out the blocks she was making for Charles' quilt. While Amanda looked at the blocks, Sarah told her some of the stories around them.

Later, they took their wine glasses into the living room. "I'm sorry I don't have any dessert," Sarah apologized.

"No," Amanda objected. "Dinner was perfect."

"Okay," Sarah began. "I guess we need to get down to business. Tell me about Andy."

"There's not a lot to tell yet, but he has an excellent lawyer. I don't think there will be a trial at all. I think this young lawyer, Michelson, plans to go before the judge and petition for the new charges to be dismissed. I'm not sure of the legalities involved, but he seems pretty sure he can pull this off."

"How is Andy? We haven't been allowed to visit him."

"No. He can't have visitors until the judge rules on Michelson's petitions. I'll let you know. But Andy is doing fine. He seems relaxed and confident that the system will be able to locate Caitlyn. I hope that's true."

"Do you have doubts?" Sarah asked, with concern.

"It's a needle in a haystack, Sarah. There are so many kids out there and so many places for them to be and things that can happen to them. Hamilton has a rough element over on the east side. We just have to hope that's not where she ends up. Men are trolling the streets looking for just that kind of girl—young, frightened, alone.

Sarah looked horrified. "I'm sorry, Sarah," Amanda said apologetically, laying her hand on Sarah's arm. "I didn't mean to upset you. I should be more careful what I say. I'm sure they'll find her."

Amanda's reassurance didn't help because the words were already out there. Clearly, Amanda hoped she would be found, but she also knew what could happen to a young girl living on the street.

"My friend over in Hamilton told me that Charles has been a tremendous help to them. He has been interviewing people living on the street and in shelters. He has actually gotten a few leads. None of them have led directly to Caitlyn," Amanda added, "but he has found people who think they have seen her. He is really good at getting people to talk to him. They trust him right away."

"He's a good man," Sarah said, looking down and blushing slightly.

"I see," Amanda responded with a teasing smile. "I see. Well, good for you."

"Okay. Enough of this," Sarah said, making it clear the subject was dropped. "What else have you found out?"

Looking serious again, Amanda continued, "There was one possible lead last week. A girl fitting Caitlyn's description was seen in the Hamilton bus station. She bought a ticket to St. Louis. No one knows if she actually went. The bus driver doesn't remember her."

"That's not good news," Sarah said. "If she left Hamilton, she could be anywhere."

"True. But it might not have been her. We'll just have to keep following leads and be patient."

"Okay, Sarah. On to your business. You wanted to talk to me. What's up?" Amanda reached for the wine bottle and refilled both glasses.

Sarah sighed and began the story of the missing quilt.

Chapter 19

The young girl got off the bus in Middletown. She had intended to go to St. Louis, but the idea of an unfamiliar city frightened her. She had no idea who she and her mother visited in Middletown but, at least, there was one thread of a connection to the town and she wouldn't feel quite so alone.

It was dark when she arrived at the deserted bus station. She didn't go in but, instead, walked up the street. There were lights and she hoped to find an inexpensive place to eat. She wondered if she could get a refund of the money she wasted on the bus ticket. Maybe she would talk to them tomorrow. Right now she needed food and maybe a place to sleep.

The restaurant she found was brightly lit and the smells were inviting. She hadn't eaten since the previous day. She went in and inconspicuously slid into a booth. When the waitress came, she asked for a cup of soup, a glass of ice water, and lots of crackers. She carefully counted out $2.59 and laid it on the table. The waitress brought the water and crackers first. When she returned with the soup, she noticed the crackers were gone. She returned with a basket of crackers, rolls, and butter. The young girl smiled at her shyly. The waitress returned the smile and said, "Let me know if you need anything else."

The girl ate slowly now, having gulped the first crackers down. The soup was hot and comforting. She wondered if she dared order a second cup. She counted her money and decided that would be foolish. She didn't want to run out of money before she figured out what to do. She was glad it was summer. She could sleep outside. The warm soup was making her feel sleepy.

The waitress smiled at her as she left the restaurant. The girl walked up the street passing several shops. They were all closed. She came to one with a strange name, Persnickety Place. She wondered what they sold.

As she was passing the shop, the girl noticed a strange structure in the back. She didn't know it was called a gazebo; she only knew it looked inviting. There was a long bench inside. No one was around. She opened her duffle bag and took out a sweater and bunched the bag up to make a pillow. She curled up on the bench and used the sweater as a cover. Within minutes, she was sound asleep and dreaming of a different life.

* * * * *

"Yes, Sarah. I'm glad you told Amanda about the quilt," Sophie said impatiently. "What I don't understand is why it took you so long."

"It's hard to explain, Sophie. I guess I just didn't want to admit that I'm that vulnerable. If someone can come into my house and take something without me having any idea it happened … well, that's disconcerting."

"Okay. I guess I get it," Sophie responded rather unsympathetically. "But go on with your story. What did Amanda have to say?"

Sarah looked sheepish for a moment, then rolling her eyes, said, "She said exactly what you said, 'why did it take so long to report it.'"

"Of course, she did," Sophie huffed. "What else could she say?" After a short pause she asked, "What's going to happen next?"

"She's sending someone over today to take my statement and look around the house. Amanda said it's too late to treat it as a crime scene, but they might notice something we've missed. Amanda took a look around and didn't see anything suspicious. There was no evidence of a break-in. Amanda said whoever came in must have had a key unless I left the door unlocked."

"Is that possible?" Sophie asked.

"It's very unlikely," Sarah responded defensively.

"Someone just pulled into your driveway," Sophie announced. Sophie never missed anything that happened on the block. "Do you want me to go with you? He's in uniform."

"Thanks, Sophie. I can handle it. I'll call you after he leaves."

The young officer introduced himself as Officer Blakely. He wrote down the details of the robbery as Sarah told it. He asked the same questions Amanda had asked: Who has a key? Do you always lock the door? Is there a key hidden outside? Have you replaced any of the screens since you noticed the quilt missing? What else is missing? When they went into the sewing room, Sarah was embarrassed to see that she had left the room very disheveled.

She showed him the oak cabinet where the quilt had been stored on the bottom shelf. "Do you always leave the cabinet door open like this?" he asked.

"Only when I'm sewing," she responded defensively.

"Nothing else is missing?" he asked again.

"No," she answered again. "Nothing that I know of."

"And when did you first notice it missing?" he asked, even though they'd already covered that.

"At least a month ago," she said, annoyed. "And I know I should have reported it earlier. I guess I thought it would show up." Sarah knew that wasn't entirely true, but she didn't want to try to explain an elderly person's feelings of vulnerability to this very young officer.

As he was walking toward the door, Sarah asked if they are usually successful in finding stolen items. "Rarely," he answered curtly and left.

"Well that was a waste of time," she said to Barney. "Let's go eat lunch." Barney wiggled his approval and they headed for the kitchen.

Chapter 20

Bea entered Persnickety Place early the next morning to clean the ice cream machine and get the shop set up for the day. As she unlocked the back door, she saw something move in the gazebo. She moved closer and realized the young girl was back and appeared to be sleeping. Bea wondered what she should do. The girl was very young and probably a runaway. *Should I call the police?* She went back into the shop, poured the cleaning solution into the machine, and turned it on so it could be processing while she decided what to do about the girl. *Maybe I should talk to her first.*

By the time she washed her hands and turned to go outside, she saw the girl hurrying away. "Please wait," Bea called after her. The girl stopped, looking confused about what to do next. "Come on back, please. I just wanted to say hello." The girl reluctantly walked toward her, looking disheveled and tired. "I'm hungry," Bea added, "and was going to walk up to the cafe for a little breakfast. Would you like to come with me?"

"No, thank you," the girl responded.

"My treat. I hate to eat alone," she added with a friendly smile.

The girl looked at the woman and sensed that she was not a danger to her. The girl was very hungry. She thought about the stale rolls she had stuffed into her duffle bag the night before. That was to be breakfast. A hot meal at the cafe sounded tempting. *Maybe even hot cocoa.* "I guess," she said hesitantly.

While walking the two blocks to the cafe, Bea kept the conversation going. She asked the girl's name and the girl said it was *Catherine*. Bea doubted that was her real name because she was hesitant, then stumbled over the word as she said it. "Catherine," the girl repeated more confidently this time, as if she decided that would be a good name.

When they reached the cafe, the girl relaxed and seemed eager for the food to arrive. They ordered cocoa and the girl drank the whole cup straight down. Bea ordered her a second cup. "Where are you from?" Bea asked, as casually as she could, hoping not to cause the girl to withdraw.

"Oh, I'm from another state. I'm here visiting my grand-mother." She dropped her eyes as she spoke and began fidgeting with her napkin.

Another lie. She's surely a runaway. I'll get a good meal in her and call the police. She needs to be taken to a safe place. The eggs and hotcakes arrived and the girl seemed to come alive over the food. She smiled at Bea and ate with gusto. She even asked a few questions about Bea's shop. Bea told her about the Christmas Room and asked if she would like to come in and look around. The girl said she would love that and rewarded Bea with a warm smile.

"I need to use the girl's room first," the girl said. Bea pointed the way and signaled the waitress for the bill.

"Sweet girl," the waitress said as she took Bea's money.

"You know her?" Bea said with surprise.

"She's been in a couple of times this week. She always seems very hungry, but only orders a cup of soup. I don't know where she lives but she's always out pretty late. She must live nearby." Bea doubted that the girl was anywhere near her home, assuming she had one somewhere. She would call the police as soon as they returned to the shop.

Bea sat back down in the booth to wait. The girl had been gone a long time but Bea decided she was probably washing up. Bea waited another five minutes and decided to check on her. The ladies room was empty. The back door was ajar. The girl was gone.

* * * * *

"Sarah," Amanda said anxiously as Sarah picked up the phone. "I'm so glad you're home! You need to get over to the court house right away. The judge wants Andy in the courtroom when he responds to the district attorney's recommendation. It's an open hearing and I knew you would want to be there to support him. Bring Sophie too, if you can. The more support he can get, the better. I have one of the guards from the prison farm coming, too, just in case the judge will allow him to speak on Andy's behalf.

"Will they want me to speak?" Sarah asked.

"I doubt it," she responded. "It's not a trial. The judge will be deciding whether to accept the DA's recommendation or if the case will go to trial. We'll let Michelson know you're in the courtroom just in case he sees an opportunity for you to speak on Andy's behalf."

"We'll be there," Sarah announced confidently, feeling certain Sophie would agree. The hearing was scheduled for the morning of Sarah's sampler quilt class but this was more important. She called Ruth and explained, and Ruth promised to save a copy of the instructions for her and offered to give her any help she needed.

* * * * *

The phone in Ruth's shop rang again. It was her brother. "He died this morning, Ruth," Jacob said. His voice sounded hollow.

"Was he at home?" she asked.

"No. He didn't make it home. His heart gave out while they were preparing him for the trip. It's merciful that he's gone. He's been in excruciating pain for months. I just wish he could have died in his own bed like he wanted to."

Ruth felt the same hollowness in her chest that Jacob had in his voice. She wondered how she could feel such pain for the loss of a father who'd rejected her over twenty years ago. But he was her father. She loved him no matter what. When she was young, she used to pretend she was his favorite and would make up conversations between them that always ended with him giving her a big smile and a fatherly hug.

"Should I come for the funeral?" Ruth asked her brother.

"Sister, it would be better for Mama if you don't come. It wasn't just Papa, you know. He was responding to the community rules and Mama needs her community right now. I think it would be awkward for her, and she is barely holding up as it is, what with Papa's death and her own illness. I'm sorry, Ruth...."

"No, Jacob. I understand completely. Just give her a hug from me and tell her I love her and I'll be praying for the family. And assure her I won't be there."

"Thank you, sister. I appreciate your understanding. And I miss you so very much. I often think of our times together, even though I was very young."

"Yes, Jacob. I miss you, too." She remembered taking Jacob down to the pond when he was about five. They fished with a string tied to a stick. When she got a chance, she would scoop up a minnow in her hand and say, "Look what you caught." Jacob would jump for joy and run home to tell Mama. *Those were good days.*

Not knowing what else to say, they said goodbye. Ruth returned to her work in the shop but the fabrics didn't look as colorful, and the sun didn't seem to be shining as bright. She held back the tears that struggled to escape.

Chapter 21

The courtroom was almost empty. Sarah and Sophie took seats in the second row behind Andy and his lawyer. Michelson was not what Sarah expected. He was short and his hair was unkempt. He wore a suit which may have fit him perfectly twenty pounds ago, but now it pulled across his back straining the shoulder seams. Sarah was sure he couldn't button the jacket. He looked at Andy like he never saw him before. The man seemed out of place in the courtroom.

The man at the table on the opposite side of the aisle was probably the district attorney, Sarah figured. In contrast to Michelson, he was dressed in an expensive looking dark blue suit with a white shirt and a red print tie. He was well groomed and spoke to the others at his table decisively.

Andy looked good. Sarah was accustomed to seeing him in jeans and a baseball shirt with his gray hair always in need of attention. He had a habit of running his hand through his hair when he was thinking, leaving it standing straight up. Today he was dressed in a suit and his hair was freshly cut and styled. Sarah wondered whether she would have recognized him if they met on the street. Of course, she knew she would know him by his kind eyes, which were focused on her now. He was able to tell her how happy he was that she came to court simply with a look. She smiled and threw him an air kiss.

"Stop that!" Sophie fussed. "You're too old for such juvenile behavior!"

"Sorry. I'll be good," Sarah responded, giggling.

"Humph."

Just then the doors opened in the front of the courtroom and the judge entered the room as everyone stood. "Be seated," the judge said gruffly. He shot a look of distain at Andy's lawyer. Sarah started to worry.

After a series of what Sarah assumed were normal procedures, the judge again looked at Michelson. He then looked at the district attorney and said that before he could rule on the recommendations, he needed to meet the accused. Michelson stood and poked Andy to stand up again. "This is Andy Burgess, your honor."

"Mr. Burgess. I have read the current charges against you. A prison break, as I understand it …"

"Your honor," Michelson interrupted. "It can hardly be characterized as a *prison break*. Mr. Burgess simply walked away from the prison."

"Sorry, Mr. Michelson," the judge said sarcastically." We will call it a prison *walking away* if you prefer."

Continuing to speak directly to Andy, the judge said, "I've read all the reports pertaining to your incarceration at Evanston Prison, Mr. Burgess. I've read comments by the guards and the administration as to your exemplary conduct. I've read the pre-parole hearing reports and it looks like you were within months of being released. What I want to understand is why you left the grounds. Why would you jeopardize all that you had going for you?"

There was silence in the courtroom. Michelson leaned over and whispered something to Andy. "I should speak?" Andy asked aloud.

"Yes, Mr. Burgess, you should speak," the judge responded. "Please come up to the front and answer my question."

Andy, already standing, walked around the table and to the front of the room. He stood at military attention. The judge said, "At ease," and Andy assumed the military *at ease* position. "You have military background?" the judge asked, raising his eyebrows.

"Yes, sir. Korea."

"Okay. Well, how about telling me just why you felt you had to walk away at that very moment."

Andy took a deep breath and began talking. He told the judge about Carrot-top and about learning his daughter had run off. He even went into the story about offering to marry Catherine and her marrying Buck instead. At one point the judge gave a little hand signal indicating he would like for Andy to get on with the relevant part of the story.

"I couldn't leave her out there with no one. I had to help her. I was going to find her and take her to my friends who'd look after her, and then I was going to come right back."

"You were planning to come back?" the judge asked in a skeptical tone.

"Yes! Absolutely!" Andy responded adamantly. "I was going to return. In fact, when I knew my friends were going to find her for me, I *did* come right back! I turned myself in."

"Hmm. Well, that's true. You did. And that's admirable. I'm inclined to accept the recommendation of the district attorney and Mr. Michelson. I guess the only thing I have a problem with is sending you back to minimum security. How do I know you won't pull off a second walking away once you're returned?" As he said the words, the judge raised both eyebrows and stared wide-eyed at Michelson.

"I can give you my word. My word is good," Andy said.

"Yes, I believe it is," the judge responded. "The reason I'm considering sending you back to Evanston is this— they've requested you back and that's very unusual. They generally don't welcome the return of their walk-aways. What I'm hearing from them is that the computer classes you're teaching are having a positive impact on the prisoners. There's a slim chance that, once these men have a skill, they just might stop using my court as a revolving door. Do you agree?"

"Yes, sir." Andy said, standing straight and looking the judge in the eye. The judge knew that this man would accept his decision, whatever it was, like a gentleman. He was no criminal and he didn't belong in the system.

"I'm going to accept the recommendation. The charges of walking away will be dismissed." He looked again at Michelson with distain. "As for your upcoming parole hearing, I'm going to further recommend that your recent actions, the walking away, not be considered in their decision."

"Thank you, your honor," Andy and Michelson said in unison.

"Thank you, Lord," Sarah and Sophie said in unison, as they squeezed each other's hands.

Chapter 22

It had been almost a week since the girl slipped out the back door of the cafe. Bea wondered what had happened to her and decided to go to the cafe and see if anyone there had seen her. She spoke with the same young woman who'd waited on them the previous week, but she assured Bea the girl hadn't been seen. At Bea's invitation, the waitress sat with her and had a cup of coffee. The cafe was empty and they sat and speculated about who the young girl might be and where she might have gone. "So young," the waitress said, shaking her head sadly.

"How young do you suppose she is?" Bea asked.

"I think early teens. She looked about the age of my sister's girls. They're thirteen and fourteen," the waitress said. "By the way, my name is Olga. I lost my name tag and haven't had a chance to make a new one."

"I'm Beatrice, but please don't ever call me that! I'm Bea."

"I've seen you around here. Do you live nearby?" Olga asked.

"No, but I work right up the street. I have that little shop in the next block, Persnickety Place."

"How do you know the girl?" Olga asked.

"I don't know her at all," Bea responded. "It's just that she slept a night or two in my gazebo. That's why I think she must be either homeless or a runaway. I was planning to call the police right after we had breakfast here last week. Maybe she sensed it and that's why she ran."

"Hmm. You never know about kids. She might show up again when she gets hungry." Bea was not as optimistic. She felt she had scared the girl off. "Please call me if she does," Bea requested, handing Olga her card.

As she left the cafe, Bea wondered what it would be like to be young and living on the street. Her heart went out to the girl even though she didn't know her. There was something very sad about her that Bea sensed. She wondered if her parents missed her. She wished she could help but knew she would probably never see the girl again.

About that time, a car pulled up and parked across the street in front of Running Stitches, and an attractive woman about Bea's age waved to her. "Hi, Bea," the woman called.

I know this woman but who … who … who. As the woman got out of her car, Bea immediately placed her as the woman who came into her shop a few weeks before. She had someone with her who bought several large bags of Christmas things, but she couldn't remember this woman's name.

The woman crossed the street saying, "Bea, It's good to see you again. We met a few weeks ago in your shop. I'm Sarah."

Of course! Bea admonished herself for not remembering her name, but appreciated that Sarah knew how important it is to keep telling people your name when you're talking to older folks. Bea knew it was perfectly normal to begin forgetting names. A friend of hers had jokingly explained that it is simply that, once you reach a certain age, your brain is so full of information, that it starts falling off the back! "Well, there must be a long trail of information behind me!" she had responded.

"Sarah! It's good to see you. What're you doing in town so early?"

"I'm on my way to Stitches. Ruth is having a sale today and I wanted to get here before the mobs arrive. I think I'm too early though. She doesn't open for another twenty minutes."

"Do you want to walk up the street with me and have a dish of ice cream, my treat?"

"I never eat ice cream before noon or drink a martini before five," Sarah said laughing.

"Well, someone once said it's 5:00 somewhere, and, by that reasoning, it's probably noon somewhere as well." The two women laughed and strolled down the street to Bea's shop.

They sat together in the gazebo eating vanilla ice cream with granola sprinkled on top since it was breakfast time. Bea told Sarah about the young girl that had slept in the gazebo a couple of nights and then took off. "Homeless, I guess," she added.

"It's sad." Sarah responded. "So many kids are on the street now and I don't understand it. Families seem to be too busy to take care of them."

"Families are falling apart," Bea responded. "It's not like it was when we were young. Remember having dinner with the family and going away on family vacations? It's all different now."

They talked about it for a while when suddenly Sarah turned to Bea and said, "We sound like a couple of old folks, lamenting the loss of the *good old days*. My grandmother used to do this very thing!" They both laughed and decided that the world would probably go on, just in a different way.

As Sarah walked back to Stitches, her original destination, she thought about the girl in the gazebo and wondered about Caitlyn. No one knew whether she stayed in Hamilton or went on to St. Louis. *Was she sleeping in someone's gazebo? Had she found a way to get food? Had she been discovered by the predators who lived off these girls?* These thoughts made her so sad she didn't feel like looking at fabric anymore. She headed home instead.

Once home, she decided to call Charles and ask him if he would like to go for a walk with her and Barney. Of course, he was delighted to do it and said he would be right over. When he arrived, he, as usual, was greeted by Barney with numerous kisses. Before they had a chance to talk about taking a walk, Barney ran to the hook and grabbed his leash. Charles laughed and said, "Okay, boy. We won't make you wait."

"But wait just one minute," Sarah called from the hall. "I want to get his new toy. It's a ball with a rope attached and I think the two of you'll have great fun with it." She hurried to the toy box where she had last seen it, but it wasn't there. She checked his corner in the kitchen, and several other places where he kept toys. It was nowhere to be found. "He must have taken it into the backyard."

"Just get his old tennis ball. He loves that too," Charles called to her as she searched the yard.

"I don't understand where it went," she muttered as she went back into the house.

Charles grabbed the tennis ball and they headed out the front door and over to the park. On the far side of the park, the town had installed a dog park where dogs could run and play off leash. "Do you feel like walking to his park?" Charles asked.

"Yes! That would be perfect. He'll love it and I'll love it if he can run off some of this energy of his. He has been getting up much too early for me." Sarah was not a late sleeper but described herself as being a slow starter. "I need my morning coffee and time to get acclimated to the day," she added. "When Barney is full of energy in the morning, we aren't a compatible couple at all." Charles pictured her sitting at her kitchen table in her gown and robe, sipping coffee, her hair mussed from sleeping and without lipstick. He smiled at her.

"What's that smile about?" Sarah asked curiously. He didn't answer but gently put his arm over her shoulder.

The tennis ball worked just fine. The guys had fun tossing and catching. Barney could actually toss the ball into the air and then catch it himself, but he loved having Charles and Sarah throw it for him. At one point, Charles and Sarah tossed it back and forth between themselves while Barney leaped into the air attempting to catch it. Occasionally, they threw it low enough for him to succeed.

When they returned home a few hours later, Sarah had completely lost the doldrums she had experienced earlier in the day. They fixed a late lunch of a hearty beef soup Sarah had made the previous day and a salad. After lunch they sat on the couch, cuddled up together and watched *Sleepless in Seattle.*

"Not many men would be willing to spend an afternoon watching a chick flick like this," Sarah said.

"I'd sit here and watch leaves falling if I could sit here with you," he replied.

They were silent for a moment, and then both laughed. "Such drivel," Sarah said, "but don't stop. I love it."

As he was leaving, they exchanged a friendly kiss.

"I could learn to love that guy," Sarah told Barney as Charles backed out of the driveway.

You already do, Barney was probably thinking as he looked into Sarah's eyes and wagged his tail. *You already do.*

Chapter 23

Barney jumped around the kitchen excitedly. "What's wrong with you, fellow?" Sarah asked. He ran to the front door and back to the kitchen. Seconds later the doorbell rang. "How can you hear things before they happen?" Sarah asked him. "Are you psychic?"

Sarah dried her hands and went to the door. "Amanda," Sarah announced happily. "I'm so glad you stopped by. I just put a pot of coffee on and I'd love to have you join me for a mid-morning pick-me-up." Barney wiggled and squirmed at Amanda's feet pleading for attention. Sarah chattered happily as Amanda came into the house, but Amanda didn't head toward the kitchen and she didn't smile.

"What is it, Amanda. You look like you lost your best friend."

"Let's hold off on the coffee, Sarah. We need to talk. Please sit down here on the couch with me." Amanda's face was tense and her eyes were swollen.

Sarah sat and Amanda took both of Sarah's hands in hers. "Sarah, I have something to tell you...."

"You're scaring me, Amanda. Please just say it...."

Amanda took a deep breath. "They found a body in an abandoned warehouse in Hamilton. It's a young girl." She hesitated, gauging Sarah's reaction.

"Is … Is it Caitlyn?" Sarah asked with a shaking voice. "Oh my. Is it?"

"We don't know, Sarah. But it matches her description. They think it might be her," she said with tears in her eyes. "They sent an officer over to pick up Buckley and take him in to identify the body."

"Oh, Amanda," Sarah cried. "Has anyone told Andy?"

"No. They won't be talking to Andy since Buckley is the father of record. If it's Caitlyn, you and I will be the ones to tell Andy."

Sarah began to sob, clinging to Amanda's hands. A few minutes later, she wiped her eyes with a napkin she pulled out of her pocket and asked, "What happened to her?"

"We don't know, Sarah. The coroner's office will let us know."

"She's so young, Amanda. And I don't think she has ever had anyone to love her. She didn't stand a chance out there on the streets," Sarah sobbed. She thought about the plans she had made if Caitlyn came to live with her. *I was going to give her the sewing room and make her a quilt. I was …*

Amanda interrupted her thoughts by wrapping her arms around her and saying softly, "It will be okay." Amanda often said this in order to comfort victim's families. But it very likely would never be okay. She thought about Andy and how his friends had assured him they would take care of Caitlyn. He was a good man and would not blame them. Still, she felt such sadness for all these good people.

"Can you stay with me for a while?" Sarah asked timidly. "Or do you need to go to Hamilton?"

"Of course, I can stay. Let's have that coffee you were talking about. Barney looks very worried about you so we need to happy him up a bit. Where's his rope-ball?" Amanda tried to lighten the mood by tossing a toy across the floor, but Barney wasn't interested in playing. He parked himself at Sarah's knee and laid his head on her lap. When she stood up, he followed closely behind her into the kitchen and sat at her foot as she poured the coffee. Her hands were shaking. His tail was drooping.

* * * * *

"I don't know why you had to come after me," Buckley slurred. "Plenty of people can identify the little bitch. Why didn't you call those nosey ladies from the school? That kid isn't my problem." Buckley sat in the back of the squad car mumbling to himself when he wasn't verbally attacking the officers in the front. His anger was clearly escalating.

"Would you just shut up back there," the officer in the passenger seat ordered. "This will take a couple of hours. Deal with it."

Buckley muttered to himself. If he was apprehensive about seeing Caitlyn's body, nothing in his words or demeanor revealed it.

It took forty-five minutes to reach the station because of the traffic. "Why don't you turn the siren on and let's get this thing over with," Buckley complained.

"Shut up," the officer responded. They pulled around to the back of the station so they could go directly into the coroner's office. They'd called ahead to say they were arriving.

"I hope they aren't going to keep us hanging around here all day," Buckley grumbled.

"Shut up," the officer responded without looking back.

There was, in fact, a very long wait. By the time the technician opened the curtain to the viewing room, Buckley had been pacing and muttering for over an hour. Officer Hawkins whispered to his partner, "This is hazard pay, right?"

"This guy better hope he has hazard *insurance* if he doesn't shut up. I'm about to bop him one."

Hawkins answered a call on his cell phone and responded, "Got it." He turned to Buckley and said, "Okay, buddy, come over to the glass. They're ready."

"I ain't your buddy," Buckley grumbled.

The technician wheeled the stretcher over to the window. The young girl was covered to her chest with a white sheet. Her skin was pale; her eye lids had been closed. Her long blond hair flowed back from her face and onto the sheet. A towel had been placed against her skull on the left side, probably concealing an injury.

Buckley stood and looked at the girl. He pulled out his cigarettes and took one from the pack. Officer Hawkins opened his mouth to object, but the other officer touched his arm and shook his head. "Let it go," he said softly.

Buckley continued to stare at the girl. She looked so young and helpless. He lit the cigarette and took a long drag. He stood motionless and said nothing. He couldn't seem to pull his eyes away from her face.

After a while, he dropped the cigarette on the tile floor and smashed it with his boot. He turned to the officers and finally spoke. "Let's get out of here. It ain't her."

On their way back, Buckley sat quietly. When they pulled up to his house and opened the car door, he didn't move. Officer Hawkins leaned down and said, "You can get out."

Buckley moved to the edge of the seat and put his feet on the ground but hadn't yet stood. He looked up at the officer and quietly asked, "What do you suppose has happened to Caitlyn?" He didn't wait for an answer. He got out of the car and, with drooping shoulders, walked slowly up the walk to his door.

* * * * *

It took another three hours for the word to get back to the department and on to Amanda Holmes that the body was not Caitlyn Buckley.

Amanda had stayed with Sarah awaiting the report. They fell into each other's arms and cried but, this time, they were tears of relief. Finally they pulled themselves together and Sarah said softly, "But she's still out there."

Chapter 24

"It's gone? What do you mean, gone?" Charles asked. "How could it be gone?" Not waiting for an answer, he headed for the sewing room and opened the cabinet door. He pulled the blankets off the bottom shelf and moved the fabric aside on the upper shelves. "It's not here!" he exclaimed.

"Did you actually think I might have missed it when I looked in the cabinet?" Sarah asked, sounding irritated. "It's *gone*, as I said."

"How long have you known about this?" Charles asked with mounting concern as he followed her into the kitchen.

"I've known for about a month. I didn't report it to the police until a few days ago because I thought it might show up. My house hasn't been broken into, Charles."

"What do you mean?" he asked, trying unsuccessfully to conceal his mounting concern. "Someone took the quilt. That means someone has been in your house."

"Charles, sit down. You're going to have another stroke if you don't calm down. Your face is getting flushed. This isn't worth it. It's just a quilt."

"No!" he said firmly. "It's not *just* a quilt! It's an invasion of your home and it's a *danger*. You could have been sleeping. You could have been killed!" His hands were shaking and his face was flushed.

"Charles, please," Sarah said as calmly as she could. "The police know about it. They checked my house, and there was no evidence of a break-in. There's an explanation for this. It probably has something to do with the key I keep outside. Someone I know must have used it and borrowed the quilt."

"That's no explanation, Sarah. Who'd do that?" Charles responded frowning. "And is that key still out there?"

"Yes, but I'll bring it in. Charles, it bothers me that you're getting so upset. You're acting like you're angry with *me* about this."

"I'm sorry, Sarah. I truly am. It's just that I worry about you being here alone, and when I realize someone has been in the house, it just makes me crazy."

"Charles, I've been alone for many years, and I don't want to be taken care of. I think I've made that clear to you over this past year. And it's the one thing I fear can come between us. I still think you're looking for a shrinking violet and I'll never be that."

"I know," he said more gently. "I don't think that's what I want. I love your independent nature and your ability to do anything you set your mind to. But that doesn't keep me from worrying when I think you might be in danger." After a short pause, Charles added more softly, "And I don't understand why you didn't tell me about this."

"Because of just this, Charles. I didn't want you telling me how to handle it, and I didn't want you taking over. I wanted to handle it myself. I would have told you if I thought you would have left the next steps up to me, but we can both see that you wouldn't have done that. You'd have insisted that the police be involved right away."

"And that would be a bad thing, why?" Charles asked.

"Because I wanted to wait," she responded. "Simply that. I wanted to wait."

Charles sighed deeply and shook his head. "I think I should leave now, Sarah, before we say things we might be sorry for. I'll call you later." He stood and walked out the door.

"What was that all about?" Sophie asked as she walked up to Sarah's open door. "He looked all red in the face. Is there trouble in paradise?" Sarah was still standing at the door looking up the street even though Charles' car had long since disappeared from view.

"I don't know, Sophie."

"You don't know?" Sophie responded incredulously. "You must know! You were here."

"Okay, Sophie. I know, but I'm not sure what's going on. I told him about the missing quilt, and he got very upset. It seemed like he was angry with me, probably because I didn't tell him sooner."

"Well sure. He wanted to be included."

"Also, I guess he thought I should have reported it to the police right away."

"Well, Sarah, you have to admit it is troublesome. You know that someone has been in your house, and you don't know when or how. Or who, for that matter. Yet you haven't seemed terribly concerned."

"Sophie, I'm concerned. At least, I'm concerned now. At first, I actually thought Andy took it. I didn't want to get him into any more trouble."

"But Andy asked you to check the quilt for a key, didn't he? He wouldn't have asked that if he had been the one who took it, would he?" Sophie responded.

"One would assume that. But what if he took it and that was just his way of letting me know it was gone?"

"That's silly, Sarah. Why would you come up with that?"

"I don't know, Sophie. I don't know. I've just always had this feeling there's more to this than meets the eye. I don't believe anyone was in my house, even though the quilt is clearly gone."

"Now, Sarah ..." Sophie began.

"Don't say it," Sarah interrupted, holding her hand up to stop Sophie's words. "I know that doesn't make a lick of sense. It's just the way I was feeling. But it's reported now. Charles knows about it now. And I doubt that anyone is seriously looking for it. That officer that was here treated me like I didn't have good sense."

"I sometimes wonder ..."

"Stop, Sophie!"

"Okay."

The two women walked into the kitchen. While Sarah took the lemonade pitcher out of the refrigerator, Sophie moved the cookie jar to the table. Barney put his head in Sophie's lap as soon as she sat down. All three remained quiet for a while. Finally Barney spoke up saying, "Woof?"

The two women laughed and Sophie patted his head and told him everything would be fine. Sarah walked behind

Sophie and patted her on the head as well. "It sure will," she said with a smile.

Later that day, Sarah still hadn't heard from Charles. She called his house, but there was no answer. She didn't leave a message.

* * * * *

"Charlie Parker! What the heck are you doing here?" Matthew Stokely was Charles' old lieutenant. The two men had been good friends before Stokely made Lieutenant and the friendship had continued, despite Charles ultimately being assigned to Stokely's department. Since Charles' retirement, they'd continued their friendship and played cards with a few other guys a couple times a month. They were the only ones left who called him Charlie. He was glad.

The two friends sat down and talked for a while. Many of the officers Charles had worked with were gone now. As he sat with Stokely, Charles felt his heart rate returning to normal. When Sarah called him that morning and asked him to come over, he had been so pleased that he neglected to take his medications. He remembered them when she accused him of being on the edge of a stroke. She was probably right. Before going to the police department, Charles had swung by his house and took his meds.

He wondered why he had become so agitated. As he sat waiting for Stokely to return with their coffee, his mind wandered back to the night his brother was shot. Jeffrey's wife, Angelina, had called and told him Jeff was in the hospital. There'd been a break-in during the night. Jeffrey always had to be the hero. He took his shotgun from the top shelf of the closet and loaded it. "I pleaded with him not to go downstairs," Angie had said, "but you know your brother." The intruder had grabbed the gun and it went off, shooting Jeffrey in the leg. The intruder ran out the back door, leaving Jeff on the floor moaning.

His brother wasn't seriously hurt, but Charles saw this kind of thing all the time on the job. Break-ins could go bad in an instant. Some homeowners simply lost belongings, some were injured, and some were dead. He couldn't separate his past experiences from what had happened to Sarah.

"Okay, old friend," Stokely said as he handed Charles the mug. "I heard you were working with Hamilton Missing Persons. What's going on there?"

"Not much, Matt. I'm mostly working the streets, talking to people, looking for leads. You know how it is. Kids can disappear on the streets and no one seems to have seen them until they turn up dead or damaged for life." Charles sounded discouraged.

"How can we help?" Matt asked.

"Actually, I'm here about a different matter." Charles started telling Stokely about the missing quilt and his friend, Sarah. Stokely interrupted his story saying, "Are we talking about that old lady in Cunningham Village who lost her quilt and is trying to say it was stolen?"

He felt his heart rate respond. "Excuse me? That old lady is a friend of mine and she's *not* trying to explain away a lost quilt. It has been stolen. This is a very competent woman and I would hardly call her an old lady." Charles was livid.

"Calm down, friend. Calm down. I'm sorry. I just saw the report and I'm quoting what the investigating officer said." Stokely had hoped that retirement would enable Charles to take life a little easier. When he learned Charles had a serious stroke, he wasn't surprised.

"May I see that report?" Charles asked.

"I shouldn't show it to you, but I will. It's right here on my desk waiting for my signature." He shuffled through a pile of reports and file folders until he found it. "Here, read it."

Charles' hand was trembling as he took the report. The officer had reported that the complainant hadn't reported the item missing until a month after the fact. She didn't seem concerned that someone might have been in the house. He added that it was his professional opinion that she was simply attempting to cover up the fact that she had lost the quilt. Twice in the report he referred to her as old. "How old is this officer?" Charles asked.

"Oh, he's a young guy right out of the academy. Why?"

"Because he seems to have a distorted opinion of senior citizens. We aren't all addled and he needs to be told that. I hope you don't send him into Cunningham Village again without some sensitivity training."

The two men sat and discussed the case. Actually, Charles was unable to defend the fact that Sarah hadn't reported the loss as soon as she discovered it. That had bothered him, too, but he certainly didn't attribute it to her trying to cover the fact it was misplaced. For one thing, she was quick to accept responsibility for anything she did. That was one of the things he loved about her. *One of the many things.* He would ask her about that, assuming she would ever speak to him again. He had come on too strong and he knew it.

On his way home, he thought about stopping at Sarah's but decided against it. He didn't want to push too hard. But, as he approached his own house, he saw Sarah and Barney sitting on the porch. He parked the car in the driveway and walked up to them. Barney was overjoyed to see him, Sarah not so much. "Hi," he said cautiously.

"Hi," she returned the greeting with equal caution.

"I'm sorry?" he said tentatively.

"Is that a question?" she asked.

"I guess the question is will you forgive me?" he asked humbly.

"I've thought about it, Charles. I know you were only concerned about me and my safety, but I just can't have you coming at me like that."

"I truly am sorry, Sarah. I didn't mean to carry on the way I did. It's just that my years on the force have warped my mind to the point that I see things other people don't see. I've seen the carnage left by the desperate people who'll break into another person's home. I'm so sorry. I just don't want to lose you."

"You're more likely to lose me by being overprotective than by the ugly things that live in your mind, Charles." He walked closer and sat down next to her on the glider. He took her hand. She didn't object.

"I'm still learning, Sarah. Please give me a chance. I care for you more than you can imagine."

"I know you do, Charles. And I care for you. I think we both need some time to think about what's happening between us." Sarah stood. Barney hopped up and stood by her side, tail wagging. "We're going to walk on home now. I'm glad you're okay"

Charles wanted to hold her in his arms, but held back. "Do you want a ride?" he asked.

"No, thanks. We need the exercise." The two turned and walked briskly up the street.

Charles returned to his car and picked up the bag of locks he had purchased, planning to install them on all of Sarah's doors and windows. "I'd better hold off on this project," he told himself.

Chapter 25

"Hi, everyone. Today we'll be making our final block and next week we'll begin putting our quilts together." Katie was conducting the class again this week. "After class today," she continued, "you might want to take a look at fabrics and choose your sashing and borders."

Katie went on to explain that her mother had gone to Ohio to be with her sister. Not wanting to go into any more explanation, Katie immediately moved to the design board and laid her own blocks out. "We have eight blocks made and one to go." As she passed out the instructions, she added, "Today we're going to make the Flower Basket block. I'd guess this has to do with carrying provisions, don't you think?" she asked.

Several people smiled and nodded and they began working on their blocks. Sarah was sitting at the table next to Danielle and her grandmother, Delores. They were talking about her high school friends and Delores was giving her the age-old advice about friends. "You're judged by who your friends are," Delores was saying. "And you know I don't approve of that girl."

"That girl is just fine, grandma. She's an A student and planning to go to college. I don't know why you don't like her. Lighten up."

"*Lighten up?*" Delores responded, straightening her back and raising her eyebrows. "Is that any way to speak to your elders?" Danny simply sighed.

Delores got up to freshen her coffee and Danny turned to Sarah, "I don't know why she gets so upset about my friends."

"Where do you go to school?" Sarah asked casually, not wanting to get into the middle of their tiff.

"I live in Hamilton over on the east side. There are a lot of wild kids in my school, but they aren't my friends. I have a couple of girlfriends and they aren't the ones that get in trouble."

"In Hamilton?" Sarah said curiously. "Do you happen to know a Caitlyn Buckley?"

"I don't really know her. She's a grade below me, but she hung out with someone I know, Britney Harris. How do you know Caitlyn?" Danny asked.

Sarah felt growing excitement. *Could it be that Danny knows something that would help us find Caitlyn?* "I'm a friend of the family," Sarah responded. "Did you know she ran away?"

"No. I had no idea," Danny responded. "But I'm not surprised. Britney told me Caitlyn was coming to school with bruises and that she cried a lot. I don't know what that was all about. As I said, I don't know her personally."

"I wonder if this Britney might know where she is. I was hoping to help the police find her."

"The police?" Danny said, suddenly looking up at Sarah. "Is she in trouble?"

"No. She's not in trouble. But she's young and we want to make sure she's safe. It can be dangerous for a young girl alone."

Danny looked thoughtful. "Britney moved and I'm not sure where she moved to. Maybe I could find out …"

"I would so appreciate that, Danny," Sarah said. "Would you call me if you find out?"

"Sure." Sarah wrote her number down for Danielle, hoping the young girl would follow through. In the meantime, she made a note of Britney's full name, just in case. *This may be our first lead.*

Sarah worked quickly on her block and rushed out of the shop just as the class finished. Once she got home, she called Amanda immediately and gave her Britney's name. "I asked this young girl to find out what she could about where Britney moved," Sarah explained, "but I decided we shouldn't wait. Maybe Hamilton can find out something through the school."

"I'll get this to them right away, Sarah. This is good information. Thanks."

* * * * *

A few hours later, Amanda called. "It's not good news," she began. "My friend just called from Hamilton and said Britney's parents haven't mailed in their request for transfer forms yet. They aren't due for another month and the secretary said she thought she remembered that Britney and her parents were traveling this summer." Amanda went on to explain that the secretary didn't remember where Britney was moving, but thought it was somewhere on the east coast.

"That doesn't narrow it down much, does it?"

"No, but they have other ways. They're going to talk with the father's employer. I'll let you know."

"Please do." After hanging up, Sarah snapped Barney's leash on and said, "Come on, fellow. Let's take a walk." As she pulled the door closed behind her, she turned and locked the deadbolt, something she rarely did when she was simply walking Barney in the neighborhood. She then stepped over to the concrete planter, tilted it to the left, and removed the extra key stored there. "I guess I haven't been as careful as I should be," she said to Barney. Barney smiled and trotted off, leading her to some of his favorite sniffling spots.

After their walk, Sarah took her quilt class tote bag into the sewing room and took out her blocks. She had the eight blocks she made in class, the one she made from the instructions Ruth gave her from the class she missed, and four more she had made on her own. She had found a few patterns in the reproduction quilt book she purchased from Ruth and had also printed out a few patterns she found online. The previous year, Andy had encouraged her to take a computer class at the center and she had become proficient at using the search engines to find things that interested her.

She decided to make one of the new blocks. The instructions online were for a nine-inch block and the ones she was making were twelve inches so she had to adjust the pattern to increase the size. "Charles would be good at this," she told herself, wishing she could talk to him.

She wondered why she had insisted on taking time away from their relationship. She had told him they both needed to think about what they wanted, but it was pretty clear that Charles already knew what he wanted. He was careful to say he cared for her, but he had slipped up once and used the word *love*. She knew he loved her; she could tell by the way he looked at her and even the way he tried to protect her. *Why am I fighting this so?*

Her thoughts immediately went to the day Jonathan died. Her world died along with her husband that day. For months she had wallowed in grief and self-pity. She had spent most of her time sitting alone in her garden. She was not herself and she never wanted to feel that way again. Sarah knew it wasn't logical to reject an opportunity to love and be loved just so she wouldn't have to lose that love someday. *And yet, that's just what I'm doing.*

Sarah went to the phone and dialed Charles number. He answered on the first ring. "Sarah?" he answered, sounding both relieved and apprehensive.

"Charles. I need for you to help me with a math problem. And also," she added hesitantly, "I need a hug."

Charles was quiet on the other end. He tried to speak but was afraid he would choke up. He was afraid to let her know how much he cared for her and how he feared losing her.

"Charles, are you there?" she asked.

"Yes, my love. I'm here and I have a hug right here I would like to share with you. I'm sorry about earlier. ..."

"Stop," she interrupted. "I was behaving badly and I'm sorry. ..."

"Let's agree to accept each other's apologies and go on from there, okay?" Charles suggested with a chuckle.

A few minutes later they shared that much needed hug on the front porch. Sophie watched from her window and shook her head. "These young folks!"

Chapter 26

"Hi, Britney. This is Caitlyn."

"Cat! Where are you?" Britney was shocked to hear from her friend. "Do you know the police are looking for you?"

"How do you know that?" Caitlyn asked with surprise.

"Some woman called my mom. She wanted to know if we knew anything about where you might have gone. She told us you took off several months ago. Where are you?"

Caitlyn was reluctant to give Britney any information. Even though she was her best friend, Caitlyn was afraid of what Britney's parents might do. "I'd rather not say," she said. "I was going to ask if I could come stay with you, but it's not a good idea if your parents know the police are looking for me. I was hoping we could tell them it was just a visit."

Britney was quiet for a moment. "My mom was very worried about you when she heard you were probably living on the street, but she said she was glad you got away from your dad."

"You told her about him hitting me?"

"Yes. I know I wasn't supposed to tell anyone, but I told my mom. We were trying to think of some way to help you, but then Dad got transferred to Long Island and we had to move really fast. Mom is worried about you, Cat. I think she might let you come here. I'll ask her when she gets home. How can I reach you?"

"I bought this cheap cell phone. I'm not sure how long it's good for, but I'll give you the number. Let me know what she says."

"How are you getting along? Are you alone?" Britney asked, unable to imagine what life on the street would be like.

"This woman has been helping me. She tells people I'm her granddaughter. She helps me find food and places to sleep. Sometimes people give her stuff because she has me. It works out."

Britney could tell a difference in Caitlyn's voice. She sounded tired and sad. "Are the police looking for you because you ran away, or are you in trouble for something?" she asked.

"I haven't done anything wrong. Maybe they're looking for me because my dad, I mean, Buck, reported me missing. I don't know why he would since he threw me out."

"Buck? Why are you calling him Buck?"

"Because he's not my dad."

"You never told me that!" Britney responded sounding surprised that her friend would keep that a secret.

"I didn't know. My mom told him that just before she left. Buck said my dad is a criminal. I don't know who he is, though. It doesn't matter. Who was the woman that called your mom?"

"Mom said her name was Miller. I don't know who she is. Mom is supposed to call her if we hear from you."

Caitlyn didn't know anyone named Miller. She wondered who the woman was and how she knew about Britney. And now she knew for sure the police were looking for her as well.

"So, I'll ask Mom if you can come, and call you back. Okay?" Britney was saying. There was a pause, and Britney said, "Cat? Are you still there?"

"Yes. I'm here. Just call me after you talk to your mom. Bye."

Mattie was waiting nearby while Caitlyn made the call. "Any luck, sweetie?" she asked.

Mattie had first noticed Caitlyn behind a donut shop in Middletown. Caitlyn was packing discarded donuts into her backpack. Mattie had always wanted a daughter, and she took Caitlyn under her wing.

Mattie had a pronounced limp and appeared to be in her late sixties, but could have easily been younger. "Life on the street does that to people," she had told Caitlyn. "Old before our time." Caitlyn didn't know Mattie's last name if she even had one. She said she had been on the street most of her life. There was a time she lived in a hospital, but it closed down.

One day, a month or so before Caitlyn called Britney, Mattie told her they should go to Hamilton. "It's a bigger town and has shelters and soup kitchens."

Caitlyn was worried about going back to Hamilton, but she was hungry and sleepy. There wasn't much help for them in Middletown. Mostly they were searching for food behind restaurants and sleeping in alleys.

Mattie and Caitlyn got a ride with a truck driver carrying chickens from Middletown to Hamilton. They rode in the back among the crates of chickens, but it was a warm summer day and a pleasant ride for them both. "Anything is better than just hanging out on the street," Caitlyn had told Mattie.

Things were better for both of them in Hamilton. They slept in a shelter every night and ate at least one meal a day at the soup kitchen. Caitlyn was beginning to get color back in her face, and the gnawing pain in her stomach was gone. There was no chance of being turned in since Mattie told everyone Caitlyn was her granddaughter.

But Caitlyn missed having a home, and she missed her friends. She even missed school. When she found Britney's cell phone number in the bottom on her backpack, she wanted desperately to hear her friend's voice. For days, she thought about calling Britney, and one day it occurred to her to ask Britney if she could come visit them. She knew Britney's mother liked her. *Maybe she'll let me stay.* She wasn't even sure where Britney was living now, but thought it was worth a try.

"So," Mattie repeated. "What did your friend say?"

"She'll call me back. I don't know what her mom will say, but I'm afraid they might turn me in. Britney said the police are looking for me."

"We can't let that happen," Mattie said. "Did you tell them where you are?"

"No."

"Good girl," Mattie praised, giving her a motherly hug. "We'll be just fine."

Caitlyn wadded the phone number up and tossed it in the nearby trash can, along with the cheap cell phone.

Chapter 27

"Well, that was some display on your front porch last night."

"Sophie, let it go," Sarah imploded.

"I will. But not forever. On another subject, I was calling to see if you signed up for the hula hoop class?"

"I did. Why?" Sarah asked sounding confused.

"Because I was wondering if you would drive us to class since I might not be able to walk home after I break my body doing this crazy thing."

"*What?* You signed up?" Sarah exclaimed.

"Don't sound so surprised. I'm just as willing as the next guy to make a colossal fool of myself. And I just might surprise you. I was quite a hula-hooper in my day."

"Oh Sophie! You've made my day," Sarah responded enthusiastically. "This will be such fun. I'll pick you up at 10:15."

Sarah studied the contents of her closet, wondering what one should wear to a hula hoop class and deciding on light weight crop pants and a matching tee-shirt. She looked at herself in the mirror and was pleased to see that the outfit looked attractive on her. She checked her hair and applied a touch of lip gloss. "I'm actually primping," she told herself with an embarrassed giggle. "I'm acting like a young girl. It must be love."

Sarah had been in somewhat of a daze since Charles left. She wondered why she had been so reluctant to allow herself to acknowledge how she felt about him. He was a wonderful man, sensitive and kind and certainly in love with her. She looked forward to their date on Saturday. He had invited her to go into Hamilton to dinner and a show. He ordered tickets to a musical that he thought Sarah would enjoy. She knew he wasn't a musical kind of guy and was doing this to please her. *Just one of the many things that makes him so special.*

"Barney, where's that new squeaky toy I bought for you? I haven't seen it all week." Barney looked at her with puzzlement. "I'll try to find it when I get home," she promised.

Seeing that it was approaching time to leave, Sarah slipped a light cotton sweater over her shoulders, took one last glance in the mirror, and left the house. Halfway down the walk, she turned around and checked the lock. "I guess his warnings are getting to me," she muttered to herself with a smile.

The instructor helped the class pick out their hula hoops. Sarah was surprised to see they weren't the ones she had seen years before, but much larger and heavier. "These are for exercise and weight loss," the instructor explained, "and much easier to use than the smaller ones." She then demonstrated how to move and where to place the hoop in order to get it going.

Sarah and Sophie stood in the back of the class, held their hoops in place, and began the swaying movement. Clank.

Both hoops hit the floor. Sarah picked hers up but Sophie couldn't reach the floor, so Sarah picked hers up as well. For the first fifteen minutes, they repeated these same steps over and over; they placed the hoop at the small of their back, swayed to and fro, watched the hoop slide down their body to the floor, and bent to pick it up.

"I see how this is great exercise," Sarah said as she rose up from the floor with Sophie's hoop the umpteenth time. "I haven't bent this much in years."

There was a sudden shriek from the front of the room as a very rotund woman lost her balance, falling over backwards. She fell into the man behind her who tried to catch her, but being very frail himself, he began falling too. The woman in the third row tried to move quickly out of the way, but her hoop was around her ankles at the time and she fell to the left into a well-built man in his sixties who was able to catch her and prop her back up. He then helped the other two get to their feet.

All three of the participants who lost their balance moved cautiously to the chairs lined up along the wall and sat.

"Bring me one of those chairs," Sophie requested. "I'm ready to join the sitters."

"You can sit down, but I'm going to master this if it kills me!" Sarah said with determination. Fifteen minutes later Sarah was swaying and the hoop was spinning. As the hoop started to descend, the instructor called to her, "Sarah, stoop down and keep swaying. You can catch it." Sarah stooped, still swaying, and the hoop was again at her waist. "Yippee!" she shouted with a laugh.

As she continued to spin the hoop, Sarah noticed Sophie shuffling toward the door. A few minutes later she shuffled back with a cup of cocoa and a Twinkie from the snack bar. The whipped cream was piled high in the cup, and with her first sip it became Sophie's mustache. Sophie gave Sarah a mischievous smile. "You were right, Sarah. This *is* fun!"

Since all the participants were older folks, there was a wide variation in ability to do the hooping. The young slender instructor made it look easy, but by the end of the class only four students were left standing. Sarah was certainly the star of the class. She was also a few years younger than most of the others.

"We'll see you next week," the instructor called to Sarah as she was placing her hoop back on the rack.

"For sure!" Sarah responded. "That was a fun workout."

"We need lunch," Sophie said as they were leaving the center. "Since we have your car, let's drive over to Barney's Bar & Grill. It's Reuben day!"

Sarah sighed deeply before she answered. She didn't want to lecture Sophie, not that it would do any good anyway. Sophie was set in her ways. Sarah knew Sophie would feel better if she were to exercise and eat healthier, but it was up to Sophie, not to her. "Okay," Sarah responded. "Shall we stop and get Charles?"

"Good idea," Sophie responded enthusiastically. "I have some questions for him about his intentions."

Sarah hesitated, not knowing what Sophie was up to. Sophie had been dancing around the subject since she saw them on the porch the night before. Charles had spent the early evening with her on the porch swing. She had to admit, they behaved like teenagers, talking, giggling, and occasionally sharing a kiss. Sarah didn't want Sophie blind-siding Charles with embarrassing questions.

"Let's keep this luncheon private, just you and me," Sarah suggested.

"Um-hum," Sophie responded, nodding her head with a knowing smile.

* * * * *

After lunch, they stopped at Stitches. Sarah wanted to see how Ruth was after her visit with her sister. Ruth and Katie were rushing around the shop, apparently rearranging everything in the store. "What's going on here?" Sarah asked.

"We're having guests!" Ruth announced with a proud smile. "My sister Anna and her husband, Geoff, are coming to stay with us for a few days." Ruth was so excited she couldn't settle down to talk to her visitors, but kept moving bolts from one shelf to another. "What do you think of this area?" she asked, pointing to a new display.

"Oh, Ruth! This is wonderful," Sarah praised. Ruth explained that it was Katie's idea. They'd picked up an inexpensive crib at a yard sale, lowered one side for easy access, and hung baby quilts on the three remaining sides. They then filled the crib with bolts of colorful baby fabric, a couple of pattern books, and a few soft cuddly toys to finish it off. "It's just adorable," Sarah exclaimed clapping her hands with approval.

"I know Anna will especially love it. They're expecting their first child." Ruth beamed as she slid one of the baby quilts over a couple of inches. "I'm going to have her choose fabric and Katie and I'll make the baby's first quilt." Ruth couldn't contain her excitement. Sarah knew how happy Ruth was to be have made a connection with her family.

"Well, Ruth, the shop is looking wonderful. When are they coming?"

"They'll be here Friday afternoon and stay through the weekend. Can you come to the Friday night quilt group? It's been several weeks since you've come and we all miss you. Geoff promised to get here in time for Anna to come to the meeting too. I want everyone to meet her."

"I will absolutely be here!" She made a mental note to invite Amanda again, although she was probably still too busy.

Sarah purchased some thread and a package of needles and the two women left the shop. After dropping Sophie off, Sarah pulled into her driveway. The blinds on the living room window shot apart and Barney's big head appeared between the slats. "Woof," he said with joy.

Upon entering the house, Sarah scratched Barney's ear quickly, and immediately turned to the answering machine to check for messages. "I'm acting like a teenager who's waiting for her boyfriend to call," she said to Barney with an exasperated smile.

Barney smiled back and wagged his tail. The two friends headed for the back door. "Let's go find that squeaky toy," Sarah said.

Chapter 28

The shop was very festive when Sarah and Amanda arrived. There was music playing and helium balloons of all colors were drifting around the room. The shop was closed to the public and refreshments had been spread out on the tables in the classroom area. "Is it always so cheerful here? I feel like I've crashed someone's party." The young woman speaking appeared to be in her early twenties and there was no question who she was. The family resemblance was astonishing.

"Sarah! Come meet Anna." It was Ruth's voice but Sarah didn't see her. Suddenly Ruth rose from behind a counter with a basket of fat quarters which had, apparently, been knocked over. Ruth moved to the young woman's side and guided her to meet Sarah. "Sarah," Ruth said overflowing with pride. "I want you to meet my sister. Anna, this is my friend, Sarah."

"Ruth has been talking about you all week, Anna, and I'm so happy to meet you. And I agree that this looks more like a party than a quilt meeting. What's going on?" Sarah asked.

"I'll let Ruth tell you," Anna said, turning to her sister.

"Well, where shall I begin?" Ruth said, out of breath. "It's all so exciting. First of all, let me tell you about Geoff. That's Geoff over there talking to Charles...."

"Wait a minute," Sarah interrupted. "What's Charles doing here?"

"Oh. Let me back up. When we decided to make this a celebration, I called you right away to ask you to bring Charles along, but you'd already left. So I just called Charles directly. I hope you don't mind," Ruth added, somewhat apologetically.

"Of course not. I'm glad he's here." Sarah responded. "So, back to the story. What're we celebrating?"

"Okay. Geoff is a computer programmer. He asked to see my website and was astonished that I didn't have one. Actually, I never even thought about it. Anyway, he's offered to set it up for me, but the exciting thing is that he suggested I also have an online store!"

"What a great idea and that'll be great for business, but won't it be lots of extra work?"

"Now we're getting to the very exciting part," Ruth added, barely able to contain herself. "Geoff works from home and it doesn't matter where he lives. They're going to move here so he can help me with the computer end of it and Anna can work in the shop."

"Oh, Ruth! That's wonderful! You and Katie will have a family operation. How exciting," she exclaimed.

"And a month ago, we didn't even have a family!" Ruth was ecstatic. The two women hugged and walked over to where Geoff and Charles were standing.

"Hi, Babe," Charles greeted.

"Babe?" Sarah responded with a grin. "Babe?" They both laughed and he gave her a friendly peck on the cheek.

"We're going to move this crib to the corner back there," Ruth explained, pointing to the patterns and thread section, "and set up a nursery here in the shop for the new baby!"

"That'll be wonderful!" Sarah responded, looking at the excitement on the faces of the new parents-to-be and the soon-to-be Aunty Ruth.

Amanda had been standing to the side somewhat lost in all the commotion. When Sarah noticed, she rushed over to pull her into the group. About that time, the members of the Friday night group arrived and were quickly caught up on the evening's happenings. Someone suggested pulling the folding chairs out into the open spaces. They couldn't form their usual circle, but what they did form worked just fine.

"Let's do show and tell while the guys are still here," Sarah suggested. Geoffrey and Charles had decided to walk over to Barney's Bar & Grill for a few drinks and to catch up on the game they were missing.

"How about you just fill us in when we get back," Charles said as they headed for the door. Sarah shot him a look but they both knew she was teasing.

* * * * *

"Hello?" Sarah said, eagerly answering her phone later that evening. Caller ID indicated it was a New York call, and she hoped it was news about Caitlyn.

"Hello, Mrs. Miller. This is Stephanie Harris, Britney's mother. I wanted to let you know that Caitlyn called here."

The previous week after getting Britney's cell phone number from Danielle, Sarah had called and spoken briefly with Britney. She then asked to speak with her mother and learned that the father had been transferred to the New York office, and that the family was living on Long Island. Unfortunately, they hadn't heard from Caitlyn, and neither Britney nor her mother had any idea where Caitlyn might go. They didn't know of any relatives other than the parents, and the only friends Britney knew of were the ones at her school and the police had already spoken with them. Sarah had thanked them both and gave them her home and cell numbers, requesting that they call her right away if they heard from Caitlyn.

Sarah was ecstatic to receive the call from Mrs. Harris. "I'm so glad you called! Did she tell you where she is?"

"She told Britney she would rather not say where she was but from a couple of things she said, Britney felt she was somewhere in Hamilton. Caitlyn asked if she could come stay with us for a while."

"What did you say?" Sarah asked.

"I didn't talk to her. I was out when she called. Britney told her she would ask me and we'd call her back. Caitlyn gave Brit a cell phone number to call. I talked to my husband and we decided to tell Caitlyn we'd send her money, and we'd let you know so you could decide what to do next."

"And … ?"

"Well, when Britney called her back, a man answered. He didn't know anyone named Caitlyn, and he claimed that he found the phone in a trash can."

"Did he say where he was?"

"Britney didn't think to ask."

"Okay. This is helpful. Give me the cell phone number, and I'll give it to a friend I have with the police department.

They might be able to track it. Thank you so much, Mrs. Harris, and please let me know if she calls again. In fact, if she calls, go ahead and make arrangements with her to wire the money. Let me know right away where and when she'll be picking it up."

"Okay." Stephanie Harris responded. "I'm just so worried about her. If you find her, please keep her away from that terrible man she was living with. She can come live here with us if she wants, but that man is a cruel drunk and shouldn't be around children."

"Thank you, Mrs. Harris. I appreciate all your help."

Sarah called Amanda right away and caught her up on what had happened with the phone calls. Amanda said she would pass the cell number and the information on to Hamilton. But before doing that, she dialed the number herself.

"Hello?" a man's voice answered.

"Hello. This is Officer Holmes calling to … "

(click)

"Damn, I messed up," Amanda muttered. The man had freaked and hung up. She called Hamilton Missing Persons and gave them the cell number and confessed what she had done. "

"Don't worry about it," the detective said. "We'll keep trying. He'll turn it back on eventually. We should be able to at least find out what city the cell phone is in when he does."

Amanda got into her squad car and headed home. She wondered if they would ever see Caitlyn again.

Chapter 29

Caitlyn wondered about Mattie's pills. In Middletown, Mattie had been going to the hospital clinic several times a week to get her medications. Caitlyn asked her where she would get them in Hamilton, but Mattie was evasive. When Caitlyn brought it up again a few days later, Mattie got agitated and said, "I don't need crazy pills anymore. Stop talking about it."

Caitlyn didn't bring it up again, but she thought Mattie was changing. She had been kind at first, but she was beginning to snap at Caitlyn. Once she didn't seem to know who Caitlyn was. "Get away from me," she had snarled.

One morning when Caitlyn woke up in the shelter, she saw that Mattie's bed was empty. She got up and looked around but couldn't find her. Mattie's cart was gone as well. As Caitlyn was coming out of the washroom, a counselor called to her, "Susan." Caitlyn didn't respond at first, forgetting that was the name she and Mattie had decided for her to use. "Susan?" the person repeated.

Caitlyn turned and said, "I'm sorry. I didn't hear you. What?"

"I just wondered if you're okay," the shelter counselor said.

"Of course," Caitlyn responded with a smile not wanting to attract any attention. "I was just looking for my grandma."

"She left a while ago, Susan. Didn't she tell you she was leaving?"

"Oh yeah," Caitlyn responded. "I forgot." She grabbed her backpack and strolled out of the shelter.

* * * * *

Sarah was coming home from the grocery with bags in both arms. She had trouble unlocking the door and dreaded the minute Barney rushed to greet her, fearing she would drop one of the bags. *And, of course, it will be the bag with the eggs!*

To her surprise, Barney didn't meet her at the door. She went through the living room into the kitchen and placed the bags on the counter top. "Barney," she called. "I'm home." There was no response. "Barney?" Sarah was getting worried. "Where are you, Barney?"

Sarah walked past her room and, not seeing him in his bed, she continued back to the sewing room. Barney wasn't there. Beginning to get worried, Sarah called again, this time with a bit of desperation in her voice. "Barney, where are you?" She went into her bedroom where, not only was his bed empty, but so was his toy box. Looking down she thought she saw the dust ruffle move. "Barney?" she said hopefully. "Is that you?"

A nose protruded between the folds of the dust ruffle but no eyes. Sarah bent down and lifted the ruffle, and there was Barney lying flat on the floor. "Come on out, fellow. What's the matter?" Barney slowly scooted on his stomach and moved to the corner of the room. His tail was down and his head drooped. He looked at Sarah with the most forlorn look she had ever seen. "Poor fellow," she said, "What's the matter?" she moved to comfort him. He curled up and turned his head toward the corner.

Looking back toward the bed, Sarah noticed the corner of a yellow toy sticking out from under the bed. "There's one of your lost toys, Barney. Have you been taking them under the bed?" She got down on her hands and knees and lifted the dust ruffle. There were about a dozen toys scattered around under the bed. In the far corner, she spotted one of her favorite night gowns. She hadn't noticed it was missing. The bed was against the wall so, rather than move the bed, she got a broom to coax it out. As the gown moved, she saw something behind it wadded up with a deep indentation in the shape of Barney's curled up body.

"Andy's quilt," she screamed. "*You* had Andy's quilt?" Her voice was loud and angry. She moved the bed quickly and pulled the quilt out. "I can't believe this! And I'm going to have to admit to Charles and Sophie that it was here all the time. And ... oh no ... I'll have to admit it to that dreadful policeman who was sure I was addled." She continued to scold Barney as she hugged the quilt like an old friend, but when she looked over at Barney, she saw he was shaking.

"Oh, Barney! I'm sorry! I didn't mean to scare you. You were just looking for a safe place to curl up when I left you alone. Come here, Barney." She held out her hands to cuddle him, but he curled up in a tighter ball. She sat down on the floor by him and softly rubbed his back and scratched his ears. "I'm sorry I yelled. That must have scared you."

Sarah had no idea what Barney might have been through when he was living on the streets, but he trusted her to provide him with a safe home. She felt terrible about frightening him. After a while, he lifted his head and placed it on her lap. Finally, he rolled his eyes upward and looked at her. She hugged him and said, "Let's go for a walk." He was a bit reluctant at first, but ten minutes later he was trotting up the street and greeting all his furry friends with a familiar sniff. All was forgiven.

But Sarah had some phone calls to make!

Chapter 30

"Well, my dear, what would you like to do for our anniversary?" Charles asked with a sly grin.

"And what anniversary would that be, my dear man?" she asked in a coy manner that made him laugh.

"Next Friday will be exactly one year since you walked into the center's snack bar and took my breath away."

"You kidder," she responded. "Really, what anniversary?"

"That's it. The day I fell in love with you."

"Oh now, come on. You didn't fall in love with me that day!"

He grinned and kissed her gently. "Well, I could have. But anyway, it's the anniversary of the day we started getting to know each other. So, back to the original question, what would you like to do?"

"You make some suggestions, and I'll tell you what sounds good."

"Okay," he said, rolling his eyes toward the ceiling as if he were attempting to come up with a plan. "How about we … oh … let's see. How about we fly to New York for the weekend and take in a show?" He looked proud of himself for coming up with the idea.

"Hmm. Well, that's an interesting thought, but how about I make a suggestion as well."

"Okay," he responded. "Let's hear it."

"How about we … oh … let's see. How about we pack a picnic and go back to that picturesque state park with the hiking trails and the waterfall?"

"You would actually prefer that to the excitement of New York City?" he asked, somewhat astounded.

"The fact is," she said thoughtfully, "I really would."

"Okay," he said. "I'm game, but you have to let me do one thing. I want to provide all the food."

"You?" she responded with astonishment. "You don't cook!"

"I might not cook, but I can sure come up with a picnic fit for a queen. Trust me," he said with a twinkle in his eye as they arrived back at Sarah's house after a relaxing walk through their local park.

"Do you want to come in for coffee?" she asked.

He pulled her into his arms and kissed her forehead. "Not today, sweetie. I told Geoff I'd meet him at Barney's to discuss some of his ideas for the shop. I don't know much about the computer business, but he seems to think it will help to run his ideas by me."

"Well, he's right. That level head of yours will be a tremendous benefit to him." She squeezed his hand and turned to take Barney into the house. Looking back at him, she felt her heart take an extra beat. *Such a good man.* He winked and got into his car.

The phone was ringing as she walked into the house. "You're making a public nuisance of yourself, necking out in the street for all the world to see."

"Now Sophie, you know we weren't necking. That was just a little good bye kiss. Now, why are you calling me the minute I walk in the door?"

"I wanted to know how he took the news."

That morning Sarah had called Charles and asked him to drop by. They took Barney for a walk and, while walking, she told him about the discovery of the previously missing tie quilt. She wasn't sure how he would react. In fact, Charles was extremely relieved to learn that it was Barney and not an intruder. He suggested they go into the police station the next morning and talk to Amanda about it. Knowing what the previous officer had written in his report, he didn't want Sarah to report it directly to him. "She'll know what to do."

Sarah told Sophie about her talk with Charles and then asked her if she would like to come over and help her check the quilt to see if there is anything hidden in it. Sophie was eager to find out and hurried right over.

"How are we going to do this without destroying the quilt," Sophie asked.

"Charles suggested we start simply by feeling it on a flat surface to see if there is anything lumpy. Then maybe we should squeeze it to see if anything crackles or crunches like something paper, such as money or a map. He suggested we hold it up to a window to see if we can spot a shape inside, but I don't think that will work. The ties are all dark and I doubt we could see through them."

"But we could try," Sophie said. "Did he have any other ideas?"

"Yes. He thought we should go over it with a magnet. If there's something metal, like a key or jewelry, the magnet should respond."

"If there's something metal we'll be able to feel it," Sophie said with authority.

"Maybe."

Together they spread the quilt out on the bed and went over every inch with their hands, feeling for lumps. They felt nothing unusual although there were a few thick spots where seams came together.

"Is this something?" Sophie asked, showing Sarah a lump where the ties came together at the sashing.

"I don't think so, Sophie. That feels like fabric to me."

"Maybe the bed is too soft," Sophie suggested. "Let's spread it out on the kitchen table." They moved into the kitchen and again went over the quilt, one section at a time.

"I don't feel a thing unusual," Sarah said finally. "Let's try a magnet."

"And do you happen to have a magnet in your possession?" Sophie asked sarcastically, expecting the answer to be no.

"Actually, I do have one," Sarah said smugly. "But only because Charles left one here when he was working on my sewing table. In fact, he left me a whole tool box," she added.

She brought the tool box out and removed the magnet. They began moving the magnet slowly over the quilt with no results until they got to the last quarter. Sarah was holding the magnet when she thought she felt a slight pull. "Wait! Let's go back." She slowly retraced her previous path up and down the fourth quarter of the quilt one inch at a time. She felt the pull again.

With excitement, she put the magnet down and began feeling. "Here! Touch right here. Do you feel something?" she asked Sophie.

Sophie carefully examined the area Sarah had located. "I think so, but it's very small. If that's a key, it's too small to open anything of any significance."

"Let's wet just that part and see if we can get the fabric to take the shape of whatever is inside," Sarah suggested. They tried it and the small lump became more prominent, but they couldn't determine for sure what it was. "But it responded to the magnet, so it must be something metal that doesn't belong there."

"Unless his grandmother left a straight pin or a needle in the quilt," Sarah suggested in a disheartened tone.

"We need to open this quilt up and see what it is," Sophie announced with far more enthusiasm than Sarah felt.

"I think we need to see Andy." Sarah said. "I don't want to pull his grandmother's stitches out without his permission."

"Let's go by the prison tomorrow and see him," Sophie suggested. "I want to go see him anyway. I was just putting it off because I know he'll ask for news about Caitlyn and we don't have any. I keep thinking we should be doing something to help find her, but I don't know what." Sarah wasn't accustomed to seeing Sophie in such a serious mood.

"I know, Sophie," she said sympathetically. "I feel the same way, but I think we've done all we can by getting the police involved in the search. They can do so much more than we can."

"You're probably right. But we promised to help."

Sarah reminded Sophie that Charles was spending several days a week in Hamilton walking the streets, looking for her.

"True. I guess there isn't anything else we can do. They will find her eventually. I'm just worried about her."

After relaxing awhile and getting some perspective on the quilt issue, Sarah spoke up and said, "I think we should put the quilt away for now. Then tomorrow I think we should go see Andy and find out if he wants us to open the quilt, even if it results in damaging it. And, if he agrees, then we should stop at Ruth's shop and ask her opinion on how to go about it causing the least damage."

"I like it. Good plan. Much better than your last plan," Sophie said.

"My last plan? What was that?" Sarah asked looking perplexed.

"Hula hooping!"

Barney, lying on his stomach with his head resting on his outstretched paws, watched the two women laugh. He sighed deeply and closed his eyes for a mid-afternoon nap.

Chapter 31

Amanda's cell phone rang. "Officer Holmes," she responded.

"This is Kanita Jackson, over in Hamilton. I wanted to let you know we got through on that cell phone number you gave us. I managed to get him into a conversation long enough to trace his location. He's here in Hamilton."

"Hamilton," Amanda responded with surprise. "I'd suspected she was long gone by now. This is good news."

"In a way, it's good news," Kanita responded, "assuming she and the discarded cell phone are both in the same city. The problem is that we've run out of leads. No one seems to have seen her for the past two weeks."

"She has been seen, though?" Amanda asked.

"Yes. Do you think you could come to Hamilton and work with us for a few days?"

Amanda arranged with her lieutenant to be temporarily detailed to the Hamilton department to help in the search for the young girl.

When she arrived in Hamilton, a city of about 100,000, Amanda was immediately discouraged. She was reminded that the city was more than three times the size of

Middletown, and she realized how easy it would be for Caitlyn to simply disappear. At the Hamilton Police Station, she was introduced to the young investigator, Kanita Jackson. Officer Jackson was assigned to the Missing and Abused Children's Division and had been working on Caitlyn's case for about a month. "Call me Kanita," the young woman said.

"And I'm Amanda." They left immediately and decided to check out all the shelters first. "We've done this before," Kanita explained, "but every day the shelter population changes and there's a chance she's either there, or has been there."

"Yes, I've seen that young lady," the first shelter manager said looking at Caitlyn's school picture. "She comes in with her grandmother. Well, let me amend that," he added. "She *used* to come in with her grandmother. I haven't seen either of them for several weeks."

Amanda and Kanita got the same response from all four shelters. "We can check with the churches," Kanita suggested, "but there are dozens of them. Let's try a couple of the most likely ones this afternoon and the rest tomorrow."

"Yes. I know this girl," Pastor Sweeney said. Her name is Susan. She was here with her grandmother about a month ago, and she just came back a few days ago by herself. I called her in to my office to talk to her about her situation and to ask about her grandmother. She's much too young to be out there alone. While I was taking a phone call, she vanished. I looked all over the grounds, but she was gone. I'm sorry."

"We've learned a couple of things," Kanita said, reviewing their progress as they slowly drove up and down the streets of the east side. "They were together up until a couple of weeks ago, and now apparently the girl is on her own."

"Another thing we know now," Amanda offered, "is that she's using the name *Susan*. I wonder who the *grandmother* is."

"No telling," Kanita responded. "… some street person who attached herself to Caitlyn. They do that sometimes. These people are usually loners but when a young girl comes along, occasionally it brings out a woman's maternal side and she tries to protect the kid."

"There's plenty to be protected from." Amanda said wistfully. "She's alone now. I sure hope she can protect herself from the sick predators out there."

The next two churches hadn't seen her, but the staff they spoke with admitted they weren't always involved with the housing portion of the program. The two officers left a picture of Caitlyn and their cards everywhere they stopped, encouraging people to contact either of them if they think of anything else or if Caitlyn comes in.

They drove through the park, but it was getting dark and they were unable to see the faces of the young people clearly. *So many young people*, Amanda mused.

Amanda got some recommendations from Kanita for a reasonable motel where she could stay for the few days she would be in Hamilton. Kanita drove Amanda back to the station where her car was parked. That night Amanda decided to drive the streets on the off chance she might spot Caitlyn. She parked in a rather unsavory part of town and went into a rundown coffee shop. She drank black coffee since she didn't trust the milk which appeared to have been sitting out all day. The metal pitcher was warm to the touch. The coffee was acidic enough to kill anything that might attempt to grow in it, she decided.

182 Carol Dean Jones

As she sat, she watched the young girls who came and went. She was facing the front windows and could watch the street as well. At one point she saw an old woman walk by with a cart, and she thought about the grandmother Caitlyn had been seen with. She dropped money on the counter and followed the woman for a couple of blocks. The woman turned into an alley.

Amanda pulled out her gun before walking into the total darkness. She snapped on her flashlight and looked around. A mass of humanity lay on the ground along the walls of the buildings butting up against the alley. There was little response to her presence. The woman she was following turned and looked at her. "What're you doing here?" she demanded in a crackling voice.

"Looking for a young girl," Amanda said softly. "I want to help her."

"Go help yourself. We don't want you here." She shoved her cart into Amanda but pulled it back, not wanting to lose her only possessions.

Amanda lost her balance temporarily but was able to keep from falling. She felt angry but didn't want to alienate the woman who was possibly her only chance of finding Caitlyn. "Will you look at a picture?" Amanda asked gently. The woman turned and slowly limped away. Amanda sighed but didn't leave right away. She shined the light into the face of each person there, rarely getting any response. Caitlyn was not there. *How many more alleys are there like this?*, she wondered.

Amanda returned to her motel room and showered. She spent a sleepless night thinking about a young girl struggling to survive.

Chapter 32

Sarah placed all of her blocks on her design board and they barely fit. She had been making extras of some of her favorites from the class, like the Log Cabin, the Bear Paw, and the Bow Tie. She had also chosen eight more blocks from her book of traditional blocks.

Since she was making Charles a Civil War–period quilt, it wasn't important to her whether the blocks fit into the various stories about the use of blocks in the Underground Railroad. She had looked the subject up on the internet and discovered that, indeed, there was much controversy about whether the story was fact or fiction. Most historians questioned its validity. But the blocks she was using were traditional and used in the 1800s and the fabrics were true reproductions from that period. She knew Charles would love it.

As she moved the pieces around on the design wall, she was amazed to see new patterns emerging. She was only vaguely aware that the pieces of her own life were also moving into new places and forming new patterns.

* * * * *

The next day, Amanda and Kanita continued their patrolling of the streets of Hamilton and questioning people likely to have come into contact with Caitlyn. The few people who'd seen her over the past month all reported her name as Susan, but no one could offer a lead as to where she might be.

Amanda told Kanita about her run in with the old woman in the alley. Kanita immediately drove to the location. It was completely empty. "We're getting nowhere," Amanda announced. "Absolutely nowhere."

When they stopped for lunch, Amanda said she needed to check in with her friends in Middletown. She went outside while they were waiting for their order and dialed Sarah's number.

"Hello, Amanda," Sarah answered, still enjoying her caller ID. "How is it going in Hamilton?"

"It's not going so well. We keep finding places Caitlyn has been, but no one has seen her lately. I'm beginning to wonder if she's still here." Amanda was quiet for a minute and then said, "I'll be coming back to Middletown in a few days."

Sarah thought that Amanda sounded disheartened. "Are you okay," Sarah asked.

"I'm okay. Just tired and discouraged."

"Come over when you get back. We'll have a relaxing dinner, play around with the quilt patterns I have here, and get your mind off of this for a few hours. Maybe a refreshed mind will lead to new ideas."

"That would be good, Sarah. But I can't stop worrying about this young girl. I'm out here on the streets looking for her, and the thought of her being out here too is devastating.

There's a reason I turned down juvenile work years ago. I just can't take it."

"You're a very caring person, Amanda. This must be hard for you."

"It's always helpful to talk with you, Sarah. I'll bite the bullet and work on this a couple more days, and then we'll have some relaxed, creative time together, okay?"

"Absolutely. Thanks for keeping me in the loop," Sarah added as they hung up.

Chapter 33

Caitlyn had been eating scraps from behind the pizzeria. She longed for a hamburger or a piece of chicken. She knew she could probably eat better behind one of the other restaurants, but most of them had tall dumpsters. She wasn't climbing into one of those, at least not yet.

The stomach pains had returned. She was bone tired and prayed for a bed, at least for one night. She was afraid to go to a shelter for fear of being turned in. She wondered what being turned in might mean. *Being placed in a foster home? Maybe that wouldn't be too bad. But what if they send me back to Buck?* She couldn't take that chance.

She longed for the times she and Mattie were able to sleep in shelters and have at least one good meal every day. She wondered where her mother was.

Caitlyn searched for Mattie for several days and finally found her coming out of an alley behind the diner where Caitlyn had spent her last change buying a cup of bean soup. She was overjoyed to see the old woman. Mattie turned right and limped up the street pushing the two wheel cart Caitlyn had found for her in someone's trash. "Mattie! Mattie!" she called, running to catch up with her. Mattie turned and looked at the girl.

"Who are you?" the woman demanded. Without waiting for an answer, she began striking the girl and screaming, "Get away from me! Get away from me!"

Caitlyn began to cry and plead. "It's me, Mattie. I'm Susan. Remember me? Oh Mattie, please remember me. I need you," she cried.

Mattie turned and limped away muttering as she went. Caitlyn sat down on the ground and sobbed. "Don't cry, little girl," a man said. "She gets like that sometimes. She doesn't mean it."

Caitlyn looked up to see an old man. He appeared to be at least in his eighties, but Caitlyn remembered what Mattie had said about living on the street. She wondered what she would look like if she stayed on the street. She felt she had already aged far beyond her years. "You know Mattie?" she asked tearfully.

"She comes and goes every few months. Sometimes she's gone for a year or more. No one knows where she goes. Sometimes she makes good sense and sometimes she's as mean as a hornet."

"I thought we were friends," Caitlyn sobbed. "She took care of me. We took care of each other." She wiped her eyes and stood up, picking up her backpack and putting it over her shoulder. She didn't mean to cry. She was embarrassed that the man saw her break down. "I'm fine," She said to him, starting to walk away.

"Here take this," the man said. He held out two twenty-dollar bills.

"No. I can't take your money," she said emphatically.

"My son came to the alley this morning and gave me a wad of twenties. He does that every week or so. It's so I won't come near his house. He says it's to help me but I know better. Anyway, what am I going to do with all this? Take one of them, at least. Go get some food.

She didn't want to take the man's money, but she couldn't bring herself to refuse. She imagined a hot meal or maybe a room for the night in one of those cheap hotels Mattie told her about. *A shower! Oh, a hot shower!* She took the money and smiled at the old man. "Thank you. Thank you. I'll pay you back somehow."

The man waved his hand dismissively and said, "Forget it, little girl. I have." And he shuffled off toward the park.

Caitlyn didn't spend her money that night for a room or a shower. But she did get two hamburgers and a milk shake. She wished she had only eaten one sandwich because her stomach ache got worse, but she felt stronger and the pain went away after a while.

A few hours later, she walked through the park and found a secluded place to spread out the jacket she carried in her backpack. She lay down under the bushes and slept straight through until morning. As she began to wake up, she thought her mother was lying beside her, but it was only a dream. She was totally alone.

Chapter 34

When Sarah and Sophie arrived at the prison, the guard recognized them from their previous visit to Bryce Silverman. Sarah was surprised he remembered them. "Don't see two nice ladies like you here that often," he explained. "Hard to forget that. You here to see Silverman?"

"No, actually we're here to see a good friend of ours, Andy Burgess," Sarah explained.

"Oh, ol' Andy," The guard said with a smile. "Nice guy. I've been taking his computer class and I actually sent an email to my sister last week. She couldn't believe it," he chuckled. He signaled for the guard to open the gate to the visitor's area and buzzed Andy's cell block. He requested that Andy be brought to the visitor room.

Since this was a minimum security facility, the visitor room was very informal. There were two couches and three or four tables with chairs around each one. There were several people visiting already. There was one guard on duty. When Andy walked in, Sarah rushed to him with her arms out. They hugged and, with his arm still around her shoulder, they walked over to where Sophie waited. Sophie wasn't one for hugs but she put her hand up and touched his cheek.

"Good to see you, old friend," she said with the slightest crack in her voice. They moved to the nearby table and sat, Sarah by Andy and Sophie across the table from him.

"It's great to see you ladies," Andy began, "but what's this all about? Is there news about Caitlyn?" His voice was not hopeful. Sarah figured he didn't really expect news about her.

"No, Andy. I'm sorry," Sarah began. "We don't have anything yet, but everyone is working hard to find her." As she looked at Andy, she remembered the day Amanda came to her with the news that a body had been found. She was thankful that she wasn't here to give Andy such devastating news. At least not yet.

"We came to talk to you about the quilt, Andy," Sophie said.

Andy looked hopeful. "Did you find anything?"

"Well, perhaps," Sarah began. "We've detected something very small, and it's metallic. Our magnet responded to it, but, believe me, it is *very* small."

"What is it?" Andy asked.

"We don't know," Sophie responded.

Andy looked confused. "Didn't you get it out?"

"That's why we're here. We don't want to disturb your grandmother's beautiful stitches, or to possibly damage your quilt without your permission. Do you want us to try to get it out?"

Andy hesitated. "Well, I'd like to know what's there, but I agree that it would be a shame to ruin the quilt. What do you think, Sarah?"

"Here's what I've been thinking," Sarah began. "Perhaps we could take the quilt to Ruth. You remember her? She has that little quilt shop over on Main Street."

"I remember," Andy said. "You take classes there."

"Exactly. Well, Ruth has experience with antique quilts and would probably know how to go about getting the item out with the least damage. We could take the quilt to her and see what she recommends."

"I'm for that," Andy said. "I don't expect the fortune that my brother said was there. I don't even expect money. But someone in my family started the story about there being something valuable in the quilt, and I'm curious to find out what that's all about."

"Okay. That's settled. Now. Sophie, I think you should tell Andy the story of the disappearing quilt. Only your wittiness can give that episode what it deserves," Sarah said with a chuckle.

Sophie began acting out the comedy of the missing quilt, the uptight policeman, and the remorseful dog. Visitors and inmates at the other tables stopped talking and turned toward the little group to enjoy the entertainment. Sophie was in rare form, enjoying an attentive audience.

As Sarah and Sophie left the prison grounds, Sophie slipped her hand under Sarah's arm in an unusual gesture of closeness. "I'm glad we came," she said with a smile.

"Me too," Sarah responded, patting Sophie's hand. "Me too."

Chapter 35

"Ruth, we have a question for you." As Sophie and Sarah walked into the shop, Ruth stuck her head up over the short divider that ran between the shop and the classroom. "But first, what're you doing back there?" Sarah asked.

"I'm making Anna's baby quilt," Ruth responded without stopping the machine.

"What's the rush?" Sophie asked. "That baby isn't due for weeks."

"Not true! The doctor said it could arrive any day now. Her Ohio doctor must have made a mistake with the calculations. Actually, Anna said she may have had the dates wrong in the first place."

Suddenly, Ruth stopped the machine and looked up at the two women. "Oh, but you said you have a question." She pushed her chair back and walked toward the front. "How can I help?"

Sarah pulled Andy's quilt out of the bag and together she and Sophie told Ruth the whole history of the quilt up to and including the search for a hidden treasure. Ruth totally forgot about the baby quilt she was working on and became engrossed in the story. "Feel this right here," Sarah said. "Doesn't that feel like something inside? Charles' magnet responded to this area when we scanned over it."

"Magnet?" Ruth seemed surprised. "What made you think of a magnet?"

"Well, I must admit, that was Charles' idea and, actually, a good idea since we never would have detected it otherwise. Do you think we can remove it without damaging the quilt?"

Ruth examined the intersection of the block and the sashing right where she could feel the small item. "It feels smooth," she said. "Yes, I think we can do it."

"I thought we could go in through the back …" Sarah started to say, but Ruth interrupted.

"No, I think our best bet is to clip these few stitches right here where the sashing meets the block. We can probably pull it out with tweezers and then replace the stitches with a tiny blind stitch and an off-white cotton thread." Ruth reached for her magnifying glass and examined the quilt more closely. "Shall we try?"

"Andy gave us permission. Let's do it," Sarah responded excitedly.

Ruth handed the clippers to Sarah, but she held her hands up and said "No, no! Not me. Please Ruth, you have the steady hand and the experience."

"Okay, but if I ruin it, you have to explain it to Andy," Ruth responded.

"He already knows that's a possibility. He's willing to take the chance."

Very carefully, Ruth clipped about a dozen tiny stitches and removed them with her tweezers. Using a small crochet hook, she carefully slipped through the small opening. "I've touched something," she said moving very cautiously. She switched to the tweezers. No one breathed. Very carefully she began to pull the tweezers out and exposed the edge of a thin metal item. As she continued to ease it out, they were able to see the entire thing: a very tiny metal key!

"What can a key that size possibly open?" Sophie asked, looking disappointed.

"I have no idea," Ruth said and Sarah shook her head in agreement. "It's very old."

"I haven't seen a key that small since I was a kid and had a diary. My brother popped the lock so the key never worked again," Sophie said with a frown. "… I sat on him," she added quietly.

"I think we have all had that brother," Sarah said with a chuckle.

"This is disappointing," Sophie said. "It's too small to be to a lock box or a trunk or anything where something valuable could be stored. I guess we'll never know the story behind this tiny key."

At that moment the phone rang in the shop. On her way to answer it, Ruth's cell phone rang as well. "Good grief," Ruth exclaimed. "Why does everyone want me at the same time?" She answered the shop phone first. She let out a loud whoop and hung up. "Anna's on her way to the hospital! The baby is coming!"

Ruth flipped the sign on the door to *closed*, grabbed her keys, and was halfway out the door before she realized Sarah and Sophie were still inside. "Come on girls. I'm locking up." She hit the lights and they all hurried outside, with Sarah carefully carrying the wounded quilt.

"Thank you for this," she called to Ruth. "We'll see you at the hospital later today."

"Thanks girls. I'm almost *Aunt Ruth*," she added with a giggle.

Driving home Sarah and Sophie were very quiet. Finally Sophie spoke up saying, "What now?"

"I don't know. Fix the quilt, I guess. Talk to Andy. That's about all I can think of," Sarah responded.

"This is quite a letdown."

"True," Sarah replied. "What did you think would be in the quilt?" she asked Sophie.

"Well, I thought there might be a gold coin or maybe a treasure map or perhaps …"

"Yeah," Sarah responded. "I was hoping it would be something that would make Andy's life better but, when you think about it, Andy's life is just fine. At least it will be once he gets back home. Andy makes the best of whatever comes along."

"It will be even better when Caitlyn is found," Sophie added.

"True. That's really all Andy wants."

Sarah drove Sophie to her door and then headed to Charles' house to show him the key, tell him about Anna, and pick up Barney.

Before she left Charles' house, he told her he would drive over in about an hour and pick her up so they could go to the hospital. He had looked at the key and said it was not strong enough to open anything of much significance. He said, in fact, that it looked like the key his sister had for her diary.

When they got to the hospital, Geoff came out to say they were taking her into surgery to do a Cesarean, but everything was fine. The baby wasn't positioned correctly for a natural birth, but the doctor wasn't worried. Within an hour, he came bursting into the room with a big smile and announce that his little daughter, Annabelle, had arrived and that mother and daughter were doing just fine.

Charles and Sarah congratulated the family and headed home, each silently remembering the fears and excitement of becoming a new parent. Charles reached over and gently touched her hand. She looked at him and smiled.

The unspoken words of love, she thought.

What the heck does that look mean?, he wondered.

Chapter 36

Caitlyn still had $14.67 of her twenty-dollar bill. Still dreaming of a hot shower, she decided to see what the cheap hotels charged for one night. Mattie had taken her to one when they first got to Hamilton, but they decided not to spend their limited funds on it. Caitlyn thought she could find it again.

Caitlyn walked up and down the streets in the neighborhood where she and Mattie had spent most of their time. She spotted the hotel on the other side of the street. Letters were missing from its name, but she recognized the rundown buildings on either side. Both were boarded up. She started up to the door but hesitated, wondering if the people who run it might call the police. She decided to take the chance.

Once inside, the squalor made her wonder if she wasn't just as well off on the street. The stench caused her to catch her breath. Again, she wondered if she should do this. "Do you have hot water showers?" she asked the man at the desk. He took the toothpick out of his mouth and stared at her. "What do you care?" he asked.

"I might want to stay one night," she responded.

"Oh, aren't we the lucky ones. Her highness might want to stay one night." The man had a pock-marked face and looked greasy, especially his unkempt hair. He wore a soiled red tee-shirt and was bone thin. His hands frightened her because they made her think of a skeleton.

"How much is it?" she asked, her voice trembling ever so slightly.

"Depends," the man said. "How much you got?"

"Eight dollars," she lied, hoping to keep a few dollars for food.

"That will get you a room with no bath and no television. No sheets neither," he added.

"Is there a bathroom and a shower I can use?"

"Yeah. Up the hall."

Caitlyn counted out eight dollars and gave it to the man. He handed her a key and pointed toward the stairs. "Third floor, 305." He turned his back to her and picked up his magazine.

Caitlyn made her way up the dark staircase and down the even darker third floor hallway. She couldn't see the numbers on the rooms. She looked for the bathroom and found it halfway down the hall. There was no door on the room, but there were doors on most of the stalls. The shower was in the corner facing away from the door. It was filthy and covered with mold. She decided she would shower with her clothes on and hang the clothes up to dry in her room.

As she walked back down the hall, her eyes were beginning to adjust to the dark. She found room 305 and put the key in the door. It opened easily, perhaps a little too easily. She wondered if it had been locked. There was a single bed and no sheets as the man had said.

There was a pillow. There were no towels, but she decided she could use a tee-shirt for a towel. Then she realized she had no soap.

She walked back down the dark stairwell, past the greasy man who didn't look up, and out onto the street. She walked to the corner where she remembered seeing a drug store. She picked up a bar of soap, a toothbrush, a travel-sized tube of toothpaste, and a candy bar. Her supply of money was getting very low, but she desperately needed these things.

Back in her room, she took everything out of her back pack and spread them out to air. She took the toothbrush, soap, and a tee-shirt with her to the bathroom and stood under the shower fully dressed, expect for her shoes. The water wasn't hot, but then it wasn't cold either. She scrubbed the parts of her body she could get to. She wanted to pull off all of her clothes and stand under the running water, but she was afraid someone would walk in. So far, she hadn't seen anyone.

Finally feeling clean, she turned the water off and used the tee-shirt to dry her feet so she could put her shoes back on and returned to her room. Once the door to her room was securely locked, she undressed, spread her wet clothes out on the chair to dry, and dried herself with the tee-shirt. She pulled on a long tee-shirt and lay across the bed intending to rest awhile. It was dusk when she laid down. When she opened her eyes again, the sun was shining. She had slept into the next day!

Caitlyn didn't know what time she was supposed to leave the room but decided to stay until someone told her to leave. She was glad she hadn't eaten the candy bar yet. She was very hungry.

Later someone knocked on the door, but she didn't answer. They knocked again. Finally, an angry voice said, "Hey! It's time to get out of there."

"Okay," she responded. "Just let me pack up my stuff." Before leaving, she counted her money. She had $3.97, probably enough for something from a fast food place. Once on the street, she headed for the only one she knew of and read the menu. She could just make it if she drank water.

She took the food and sat down at a booth in the back. *I've got to figure out what I'm going to do.* She knew she couldn't continue this way and was seriously considering turning herself in to the police. *I'll just let them do whatever they want with me except take me back to Buck.*

The idea of being returned to Buck frightened her so much she knew she wouldn't take the chance. She would just stay in the street until something happened. Surely something good would come along sometime. Maybe Mattie would come back and get her.

She walked over to the park in case Mattie was looking for her. The old man with the twenty-dollar bills was there again. "Hi, there," he greeted her. "I was wondering what happened to you."

"I'm fine," she responded.

"My son is coming again today and he'll be bringing more money. He'll give you some too I'm sure. Come on over to Second Street with me and I'll introduce you to him."

Caitlyn had the same feeling she had in the bus station several months before. This didn't feel right. She didn't answer him, but her body seemed to know what to do on its own. She turned and ran as fast as she could. She ran and ran until she didn't recognize anything around her.

She was in a different part of town—a part she had never seen before. There were large houses with soft green lawns. She finally stopped running and discovered she was so out of breath she was wheezing.

She was dry and needed a drink. She spotted the entrance to a park on the other side of the street and headed that way. She saw a water fountain and benches. She got a long cool drink and sat on a bench. She wished she could comb her hair so she didn't look so out of place in this neighborhood. She would like to stay here. She knew she would at least spend the day in this paradise.

Chapter 37

Sarah and Charles were driving back from the prison. It was a warm summer day and Charles had put the top down on his convertible. With the wind in her hair and her head thrown back laughing, Charles thought she looked like a young girl. He reached over and squeezed her hand.

They drove on quietly enjoying the day and each other's company. After a while Sarah spoke, asking Charles if he thought it was realistic that Andy might be released at his next parole hearing. "If he does what he said he's going to do, I think it's a done deal." Andy had a plan for continuing the men's computer training after he was released. Although he was eager to be free, he didn't want to leave the men in the middle of their training. He was thinking about offering to return once a week to conduct the classes.

"I hope so," Sarah responded. "It will be good to have him back in the neighborhood." Sarah and Charles had driven up to the prison to show Andy the key and get his opinion about it.

"I have no idea," Andy had said, "but it can't be for much. It's too small."

"If your grandmother sewed it into the quilt and then specifically gave it to you," Sarah had pointed out, "then she must have also given you what it opens. Right?"

Andy agreed with her logic but said he couldn't think of anything she had given him. Then he remembered the two cedar chests in the attic. She had several specific bequeaths in her will. Andy was to have the Tie quilt and the two cedar chests. Both chests had been stored in Andy's attic since her death.

"Did you ever open them?" Sarah had asked.

"I took a quick look. There were several quilts and some old jewelry of hers. I think there were some books, stuff like that. The chests weren't locked and, even if they were, that little key wouldn't have opened them."

Before they left, Andy told Sarah to use the key she had to his house and take Charles or Sophie with her and go up in the attic. "The two chests are sitting together on the back wall. Pull the cord to turn the light on. I poked through them right after they were delivered, but I didn't pay much attention to what was inside. I never understood why she wanted me to have them."

As they were driving home, Sarah asked Charles what he thought about them being the ones to check out the chests in Andy's attic.

"It's fine with me," he responded, "if that's what you want to do. What're you thinking?" he asked as he parked in front of Sarah's house and turned toward her.

"I'm thinking about this woman going to such lengths to sew that key inside the quilt and then to have specific bequests in her will that give the quilt and the chests to Andy. She had a plan and a reason for that plan."

"Yes," Charles responded. "She clearly had something in mind. ...."

Sarah continued, "... and her plan was *not* for you and me to go rummaging through the chests and discover whatever it was that was so valuable, at least valuable to her. She wanted Andy to do that."

"I see where you're going," Charles said thoughtfully. "Perhaps we should save this task for him. Even if he doesn't get out at this next parole hearing, he'll certainly be back home soon."

"And who knows, Caitlyn might be back home soon as well. They could be doing this together," she said with a hopeful smile.

"So what do you want to do?" he asked. He admired this good woman for her sensitivity. She was absolutely right about the key. This was a job for Andy and, hopefully, Caitlyn.

"I want to put the key in a safe place and keep it for Andy and his daughter!"

"Good plan," Charles said but then added with a mischievous grin, "but don't put it where Barney can drag it under the bed."

"Oh, you!" she said, gently slapping his arm. "Don't make fun of me." She reached over and gave him a light kiss and got out of the car. He smiled at her with love in his eyes as he turned off the car and followed her inside.

Barney met them at the door, looking just a bit peeved at having been left behind. Charles got him into a tussle on the floor and all was forgiven. After lunch, Charles explained that he had some chores to take care of and that he would call her later.

Barney followed him to the door and stood at the window watching him drive away. Sarah heard a small whine coming from the front window. "I know, Barney. I miss him too."

* * * * *

Charles pulled up in front of Kendra's Katering. He had a two-thirty appointment with Kendra to plan the Friday picnic. He had convinced Sarah he could provide all the food but, of course, he couldn't do it alone. He spent a few minutes describing the setting and what he had in mind. Kendra asked if they would need a collapsible table, but he said there were picnic tables scattered throughout the park.

He said his main concern was that she provide containers which would keep the food cold for at least two hours after he picked it up. He also said he needed to be able to carry everything about a half mile back to the waterfall area. Kendra assured him she could provide a push cart with large wheels that would work fine on the nature paths in the park.

They sat down with the menus and began planning the meal. Kendra explained that an elegant picnic didn't include hot dogs and potato salad. She suggested a papaya mango salsa diced small enough to eat on a chip. She then suggested an elegant meat and cheese platter with an arrangement of sliced goat cheese, a small round of brie, thin sliced cheddar, an assortment of thin sliced smoked meats, and a variety of crackers, miniature croissants, and finger breads.

And with that, she recommended a simple salad of baby greens, feta cheese, green grapes, mandarin oranges, slivered almonds, and a balsamic vinaigrette dressing. In addition, she would include a nice bottle of wine, wine glasses, linen napkins, silverware, and a table covering. "In this case, I'd suggest one of our picnic quilts," she added.

Charles was overwhelmed and said this was just what he wanted. Kendra said she would supply everything. She asked if he would like wait staff to accompany them, but he wanted this to be private. He was willing to do whatever was needed to set it up. She assured him everything would be completely prepared and ready to place on the table. She suggested bottled water in case it was a hot day.

"By the way," she added, "do you want a light dessert?"

"That would be nice. What do you suggest?"

"How about fresh strawberries and a chocolate dipping sauce?"

"Perfect," he responded with a grin. "I'll pick it up at 10:00 a.m. on Friday."

He handed her his credit card, expecting her to enter an amount equal to the national debt. And she did.

Chapter 38

It was dusk. It had been a warm day with a light breeze and Caitlyn had been enjoying the park most of the day. A German shepherd had wandered in from one of the adjacent houses. He checked out Caitlyn cautiously wagged his tail, and leaning down with his bottom high in the air, he invited her to play. Caitlyn took a pair of socks out of her backpack and tied them in a tight knot. She then threw her make-shift ball as far and she could and the dog instantly retrieved it. His whole body was wagging as he waited for her to throw it again. It made her laugh and the sound startled her. *How long has it been since I laughed?*

Caitlyn got up from the bench and walked with the dog. She let him lead her to all his special spots. She followed him down a hill and suddenly he disappeared through a hole in the fence. She stopped. He immediately came back and looked at her, barked an inviting bark, and ran back and forth clearly asking her to follow. She decided to go ahead and follow him.

With him in the lead, she tromped through a wooded area which suddenly opened to a manicured backyard. There were flower beds along the edges and a large slate patio with plants in large pots. There was a large table with six or eight chairs around it and two padded lounge chairs. On the far side of the patio, she spotted a brick barbeque pit. *A happy family lives here.* Caitlyn often imagined that houses she looked at were filled with happy families, especially in the evening when she could see the lights on inside. They always looked warm and happy. She was too young to realize that looks could be deceiving.

The dog was lying just outside his spacious dog house. There were blankets inside and a large water bowl by the door. The dog lay stretched out proudly in front of his house. Caitlyn looked at him and thought he was smiling at her.

It was dusk and someone called, "Jake, come eat." The dog jumped up, paused a moment to look at Caitlyn, then ran to the side door. Someone let him in. Caitlyn crept behind the dog house and waited. No one came outside. As night fell, she began to feel chilly. She hadn't eaten since breakfast but had learned not to think about it. She crept inside the dog's house, curled up in the blankets and fell asleep.

She jumped up in shock when she felt her face being licked. She laughed and put her arms around the large dog that was now in the dog house with her. She heard people talking outside and moved to the far corner of the dog house and curled up as small as she could get, pulling the blankets over her. Jake saw this as a fun game and began tugging on the blankets. "Stop!" she whispered but he continued the game. Someone came up to the shelter and poured fresh water in Jake's bowl. "Come on out, fellow," the woman called. Jake went out and Caitlyn could hear the woman talking to him as they walked around the yard.

After the woman went into the house, Caitlyn slipped out of the dog's house and ran through the woods back to the hole in the fence and into the park. Jake didn't follow her. Caitlyn sat on the bench and thought about her situation and decided she couldn't live in this part of town. There were no restaurants with scraps and no people she could ask for loose change. The first time she had done that when she was with Mattie, it had been humiliating. She had gone into a nearby alley and cried. But it got easier, especially when she was hungry. She decided to retrace her steps and return to the part of town Mattie had told her was safest.

It felt a little like coming home when she crossed the foot bridge and walked past the Fifth Street Shelter. Suddenly she knew what she should do. She decided to start spending her nights in the shelters and eating at the nearby church soup kitchens. If she got caught, she would just have to deal with it. She couldn't keep wandering around like a lost waif with this gnawing pain in her stomach. She went straight to the nearest soup kitchen and mentally thanked Mattie for teaching her where they were. That night she went to the Fifth Street Shelter and waited for a woman and her children to go in. She slipped in with them and found a cot nearby. No one paid any attention to her.

Caitlyn spent a week following this pattern. As before, she got stronger, the pain in her stomach got weaker, and her color returned. But she continually waited for the other shoe to drop.

Chapter 39

"It's a perfect day for a picnic," Sarah exclaimed as they drove south toward the state park. Charles had picked up the food cart from Kendra's Katering and stashed it away in the trunk of the car. The top was down, the sun was shining, and the sky was blue.

Sarah was wearing white knee-length shorts and a blue tee-shirt that accented her deep blue eyes. She wore a long white scarf around her neck which trailed behind her as they drove. Charles took his eyes off the road for a moment and basked in her relaxed, confident beauty. She caught him looking and smiled.

It was Barney's first ride in Charles' car with the top down. He was nervous at first and stayed on the floor in the backseat with his long muzzle stuck under Sarah's seat. After a while, he sat up but remained on the floor. By the time they were halfway there, he was up on the back seat with his ears flying in the wind.

As they pulled into the park, Barney started wiggling and whining to get out. He remembered his first visit here when he was allowed to play in the waterfall. Charles snapped his leash on and helped him out of the car. He then helped

Sarah out and handed her the leash. "This will be your job today. I have a little something that will keep my hands full."

"The picnic basket?" Sarah asked. Charles had volunteered to bring the picnic food and she had instructions to just bring herself and Barney. When he opened the trunk, she gasped. "What's all that?" she asked astonished by the size of the cart.

"It's not all food. We have accoutrements as well." Kendra had been right when she said he could easily push the cart on the nature path. They started up the path toward the waterfall, all three excited about the adventure. Sarah stared at the cart, wondering what it could possibly contain. It appeared to be enough for a sizeable group.

The path had sections where it was uphill. Charles tried to look casual as he pushed the cart. He hoped Sarah didn't notice that it was becoming a challenge. When they arrived at the waterfall, they chose a table not far from the water's edge. It had been raining the previous week, and the foliage was a lush green. Barney stood and stared longingly at the water. "Be patient, young man," Charles assured him.

Charles unzipped the bag and removed the first item. It was a brown and green quilt in a leaf pattern. Sarah rushed over to look at it and smiled knowingly when she recognized the signs of a mass-made imported quilt. "But pretty," she added. She helped him spread it out on the table. Next he removed crystal wine glasses, water glasses, a bottle of chilled wine, and several bottles of sparkling water.

As he began removing the food, Sarah exclaimed, "Oh my, how chic. Now don't tell me you did all this. I know better. How did you come up with such an elegant spread?"

Charles continued to pretend he had prepared it all but finally laughed and told her about Kendra's Katering.

At the bottom of the bag, Charles saw another container he didn't expect. He pulled it out and opened it to find a dog bone lying on top of a container of what appeared to be chicken stew. He remembered mentioning the dog to Kendra and was very pleased she had remembered him. Charles had forgotten to include Barney in his meal planning.

Sarah took Barney's leash off and told him to stay nearby. He tested the limits several times, but Charles firmly said, "Barney, *no!*" and Barney ran back to the picnic table. Charles and Sarah took their time with the food, sampling this and that, and sipping the wine. "The food is excellent," Sarah commented, clearly enjoying everything Kendra had included. Charles would probably have enjoyed a big steak. The food was a little *girlie* for him, but he didn't say so. He knew Sarah wouldn't like that comment, and he also knew the meal was perfect for her.

They clipped the leash back on Barney and took a little walk to the top of the waterfall. It was a steep climb but it was worth it. Looking down, they could see their picnic site, the water gently flowing over the rounded rocks, and a little squirrel timidly approaching their table. Barney quickly led the way back to the table and the squirrel was long gone before they got there. "We have one more course," Charles said, as he pulled out a thermos of coffee, two mugs, and the strawberries.

"A perfect end to a perfect meal," Sarah said taking his hand as they sipped their coffee. Later, Barney played in the stream and Sarah sat on the bank with her feet dangling in the cool water. Charles sighed and wondered how this day could possibly be any more perfect.

"Where's Barney?" Sarah called to Charles as he was packing up the remains of the picnic.

"He's over …" he looked in the direction he had last seen Barney, but didn't see him. "Barney," he called walking toward the wooded area where he had been playing. Sarah dried her feet with one of the kitchen towels Kendra had sent along and slipped into her shoes.

"Barney," Sarah shouted. "Barney, come!"

As Charles approached the wooded area, he heard rustling in the underbrush. "Barney, is that you?" he called. "Barney, come here!" He heard more rustling and suddenly Barney burst out of the thicket. He jumped around excited and ran back in. "Barney, come here," Charles demanded. Again, Barney burst out and ran right back in.

"He's acting like he wants me to follow him," Charles called to Sarah. "I think I will."

"Be careful back in there," Sarah said. "That thicket looks thorny. What do you suppose is wrong with him?" Sarah looked worried.

"It's okay, hon. I'll go get him. You stay there." He followed Barney's trail a few hundred feet into the brush. He could hear Barney whining. "What's the matter, boy?" he asked as he caught up with the dog. Barney's head and tail were close to the ground and there was a low sound coming from deep inside him. It wasn't a growl nor a whine, but something in between. As Charles got close, he reached for Barney's collar. As he pulled Barney close, a limb fell to the side exposing a green blanket stuffed into the thick underbrush. A woman's foot protruded from the blanket. "Stay back there, Sarah," he shouted. "I have Barney." Before moving, he pulled his cell phone from his pocket and dialed 911.

* * * * *

Charles held Sarah in his arms as the police worked. She was shivering despite the warmth of the day. He wanted to take her home, but the investigating officer asked them to stay until they could make their report.

Charles took Sarah and Barney down to the parking lot and got them settled in the car. What had been serene parkland earlier was now crawling with police cars and emergency vehicles. The medical examiner arrived while Charles was loading Kendra's cart into the trunk.

Charles told Sarah to wait in the car with Barney while he went back to speak to the officer. He put the top up so Sarah would feel more secure, and returned to the crime scene. He explained to the officer that Sarah was in shock, and he requested permission to take her home. He agreed to meet the officer at the police station later.

Charles held Sarah's hand as they drove home in silence. He looked over and saw tears running down her face. Their perfect day had come to a dreadful end.

Chapter 40

The body was readily identified as that of Catherine Buckley. Her prints were on file from her many years living on the street. Her husband, Daniel Buckley, who was also in the system as a result of numerous domestic dispute arrests, begrudgingly identified the body and was later interrogated extensively. There was insufficient evidence to charge him, although he was their prime suspect. Detectives interviewed the neighbors and Buckley's employer. The same judge who dismissed Andy's case was approached for, and signed, a search warrant for the Buckley home.

Buckley was asked to wait outside while the officers searched the house. He was angry and belligerent but ultimately sat outside on the curb until the search was complete. The search team left with boxes of personal items along with sealed evidence bags collected by the forensic team. Blood splatter had been detected in the garage, along with evidence that bleach had been used in a slipshod attempt to clean it up.

The Lab completed the blood splatter analysis and determined it to be the blood of Catherine Buckley. Evidence was still circumstantial, but a decision was made to arrest Daniel Buckley.

* * * * *

Caitlyn ran into Mattie on the street and found her to be much more coherent. She didn't ask if she were back on her medications. She didn't want to upset her. They went into the soup kitchen together and enjoyed a rich beef stew with rolls and iced tea. Later, they left smiling and with their stomachs full. Caitlyn wondered how a person could go to such extremes. *Does living on the street cause that?* she wondered. *Will I be like that some day?*

As they walked down the street, Caitlyn came to an abrupt stop. What had she seen out of the side of her eye? *Her mother?* She went back to the news stand and there, on the front page, was a picture of her mother. WOMAN FOUND DEAD IN STATE PARK. She grabbed the paper and began reading the article. She couldn't believe it was actually her mother. Tears ran down her cheeks. "What's wrong, girl?" Mattie asked. "Read it to me."

Caitlyn had trouble focusing on the words and her voice cracked, but she began reading. "The body of Catherine Buckley, wife of Daniel Buckley, was discovered in Wrigley State Park by a couple picnicking nearby. Although cause of death has not yet been released by the medical examiner, investigation is underway. Her husband, Daniel Buckley, is being questioned as a person of interest. Catherine Buckley's daughter has been missing for three months. She's currently being sought by detectives from the Division of Missing and Abducted Children. Anyone with information regarding the young girl's whereabouts should contact Hamilton Police Department."

"*He killed her!*" Caitlyn shouted. "He killed my mother! She didn't run off ... he killed her." Caitlyn began to sob. "I should have helped her. I knew he was angry enough to kill her."

Mattie looked around wondering what to do. She didn't know how to comfort another person. She had never been comforted herself, but she knew something needed to be done. The beat cop walked up to them and said, "What's the problem here?" He ignored most disturbances in this part of town, but the young girl was sitting on the ground sobbing.

Mattie handed the paper to him. "That's her mom," she said. "Help her." Mattie turned and walked off pushing the cart Caitlyn had found for her. She never looked back. The officer called for assistance and helped the girl to a nearby bench. He sat with her until the squad car arrived.

A young officer with short dark hair and kind eyes walked up to Caitlyn and put her hand out. "Hello, Caitlyn. My name is Amanda Holmes."

Chapter 41

Sitting on his porch watching the storm, his thoughts drifted back to another stormy night. It was been raining that night too. When he arrived at the park, it was close to 3:00 a.m. The moon was only in its first quarter. It was so dark he couldn't see the path. It worried him that he was leaving boot prints but, hopefully, the rain would wash them away. The load he carried was extremely heavy but he was strong. *Dead weight.* He snickered at the thought.

He left the path and headed into the brush. He had worn a heavy coat and gloves and was able to push his way through the thicket until he was far from the visitor's areas. He could hear water in the distance. Years before, when he was a child, he had been to the park with his grandparents. He knew the sound was from the waterfall. He was getting tired and decided to stop.

He had taken a shovel with him but couldn't carry the bundle and the shovel at the same time. He left it in the truck and decided not to bury the bundle. It was wrapped in an old thermal blanket the man knew couldn't be traced. He shoved the bundle deep into the thicket and piled lose limbs and branches over it. It would be found some day, but that didn't concern him.

He had retraced his steps to the truck and returned home. Later that night, there was a severe thunderstorm and he had smiled, imagining all evidence of his visit washing away.

But that was months ago, and now he once again sat on the porch watching the rain.

From a distance, he heard the blaring of sirens. Headlights seemed to be swarming around the house; in fact, there were only two squad cars. Four uniformed men got out and walked toward him, hands resting on their weapons. Buckley took a sip of his beer and remained calmly sitting as they approached the porch.

"Daniel Buckley. You're under arrest for the murder of your wife, Catherine Buckley. You have the right ..." and the officer droned on, but Buckley was no longer listening. He slipped the revolver up to his temple and pulled the trigger.

Chapter 42

Sarah and Charles arranged a simple memorial service for Catherine at the local chapel. Except for Caitlyn, there was no family to attend. Caitlyn, however, was surrounded by her new friends. Even Danny was there with her grandmother. Ruth and Katie were there, of course, and Anna came with her husband, Geoff, and their new baby, Annabelle, who cooed when Caitlyn picked her up. "She's so soft and she smells so good," Caitlyn said quietly, cuddling Annabelle protectively in her arms. Sophie arrived decked out in her new purple coat and a matching hat decorated with red plumes.

Despite the gravity of the situation, Caitlyn was handling it well. She seemed to enjoy getting to know her new friends. She was especially pleased to have an old friend with her for support. Britney's father had a scheduled trip back to the home office, so he brought Britney along for a brief visit with Caitlyn. They had been sharing the futon in Sarah's sewing room which was now called Caitlyn's Room. Sarah knew it would be temporary since Andy was scheduled for his parole hearing, and the parole officer and Andy's lawyer agreed that he was likely to be released. Once he returned home,

Caitlyn would be moving up the street with her dad. There had been no problem establishing paternity and updating Caitlyn's records.

Buck, on the other hand, had no friends. His only sister came to town to arrange for the burial and to close out his house. Sarah met her when she went to pick up the rest of Caitlyn's things. The sister told Sarah she was not surprised about any of the things Buck had done. She said he had been a very disturbed child and had been in trouble all his life. They talked briefly about his suicide. His sister thought it was from guilt, although he had never shown signs of feeling guilty about anything. "But he loved Catherine," she had said. "She was probably the only thing he ever cared about."

After Catherine's memorial service, the group congregated at Sarah's house where the kitchen countertops were filled with casseroles. Ruth and Katie were setting dishes out buffet style while Charles opened a folding table in the corner for drinks. Geoff volunteered for bartender duty, although most of the visitors were drinking sodas.

The tone in the room was upbeat and Caitlyn was smiling at Sarah when the back door opened. They both looked toward the door and saw Andy entering. "Andy," Sarah cried and quickly crossed the room to greet him. "Thank goodness you were able to come," she said as she hugged him. "Come meet your daughter."

With tears in his eyes, he put his hand out to shake the young girl's hand. She placed her small hand into his and, also with tears in her eyes said, "Hi, Papa."

Chapter 43

A *week later ...*

Andy, holding the small key Sarah had given him, looked at the covered hole on the ceiling of his hallway. "How do we get up there?" Caitlyn asked.

"Nothing to it," Andy responded. He removed the cover to the attic entrance and pulled the cord that lowered the telescoping attic staircase.

"Is this safe?" she asked, a bit nervous about climbing the temporary staircase.

"Absolutely safe!" Andy assured her. "You start up and I'll be right behind you." Placing his hand gently on her shoulder, he said, "Just take one step at a time," a philosophy that had served him well over the last fifteen years.

Together they ascended the stairs and entered the small attic. On the far wall were the two cedar chests that had been sent to him by his grandmother's executor.

Andy and Caitlyn carefully opened the first chest and found four beautifully embellished quilts. "These are works of art," Andy said, handling them carefully and setting each aside as they reached for the next one. "We'll show these to Sarah."

"I love this one," Caitlyn said, hugging a pink and yellow quilt to her chest. "See the butterflies, Papa?" She loved saying the word *Papa* and he loved hearing it. She didn't know why she chose that particular name for him. It just came to her when she saw him for the first time in Sarah's kitchen.

"Would you like to put that one on your bed?" Andy asked.

"Could I?" she responded with surprise. "Is it really okay?"

"Honey, these quilts are all yours. You can do anything you want with them."

Caitlyn giggled with pleasure. "Let's look in the other chest."

As they opened the second chest, the smell of *old* wafted out. The three quilts in this chest looked much older. Andy wished he knew who made them. He would check them later and, hopefully, whoever created them took the time to make labels.

Below the third quilt, they found a small box. Andy picked it up carefully and looked at it. It had a rusted keyhole which he hoped still worked. He took the small key from his pocket and slipped it into the keyhole. When he turned it, the top of the box snapped open.

Caitlyn leaned over him to peer into the box. Inside they saw a small item carefully wrapped in yellow silk. It was tied with a white silk ribbon. Under the small package was an envelope.

Andy carefully opened the envelope and removed the sheet of fine linen paper that was enclosed. He carefully unfolded it and saw that the letter was addressed to him.

"Read it, Papa. Read it," Caitlyn pleaded bouncing up and down with excitement.

Andy cleared his throat and began reading:

My dear grandson, Andy Burgess,

If you are reading this, then you know I have joined my maker. All my earthly worries are behind me.

One of my biggest worries, I'm passing on to you.

The ring in this box belonged to my grandmother Abigail Adams who married your great-great-grandfather Calvin Cox in the summer of 1858. Calvin had this Early Victorian engagement ring made for Abigail in England while he was completing trade negotiation with Britain. The snake was a sign of eternal love and this ring is a replica of the Victorian snake and emerald engagement ring Albert gave to Queen Victoria. It is priceless.

My grandmother Abigail entrusted this ring to her daughter, Harriet Cox, my mother, who, in turn, entrusted it to me. As you know, I had no girls. Rather than pass the ring to my son's wife, your mother, I chose to keep it for another generation. But, as luck would have it, my son as well had no girls. My heirs are you, Andy, and your brother George.

Now, as much as I am reluctant to put this on paper, I feel your brother George is a ne'er-do-well and always will be. He would sell the ring and fritter the money away.

I am, therefore, passing this ring on to you and trusting that you will hold it for the first girl in our family line. My hope is that you, my dear grandson, will produce that girl who will, one day wear Abigail Adams' treasured ring.

With love and admiration,

Your grandmother, Cora Burgess

Andy slipped his arm around his daughter's shoulder and said to the absent Cora Burgess, "I'd like you to meet my daughter, Grandma. This is your great-granddaughter, Caitlyn Burgess. She will wear Abigail's ring with pride one day."

Caitlyn kissed her father's cheek and said, "I love you, Papa."

TIME PASSES

See full quilt on back cover.

PROJECT

Sarah fell in love with the Civil War-reproduction fabrics in Ruth's shop and used them for a scrappy Hourglass block quilt. Make this 45˝ × 60˝ quilt with a combination of your favorite fabrics.

MATERIALS

Fabric scraps: Each at least 4˝ × 4˝, to total 5 yards

Backing: 3 yards

Batting: 53˝ × 68˝

Binding: ½ yard

Tip ‖ Save time by using 1 pack of charm squares (precut 5˝ × 5˝ squares). Trim the Hourglass blocks to 4˝ × 4˝ and the finished quilt will be 63˝ × 84˝. You'll need ⅝ yard of binding fabric, 5⅛ yards of backing fabric, and a 71˝ × 92˝ batting.

Tip ‖ Choose an equal number of light and dark fabrics to create the best Hourglass design.

Project Instructions

Seam allowances are ¼". HST = half-square triangle.

MAKE THE BLOCKS

1. Cut 432 squares 4" × 4", half of them light and half of them dark.

2. Draw a diagonal line from one corner to another on the wrong side of 216 light squares.

3. Pair light squares, right sides together, with dark squares. Sew ¼" away from both sides of the drawn line on each pair.

4. Cut on the drawn line. Press toward the dark. You now have 2 HSTs for each original pair.

5. Draw a diagonal line from one corner to another through the seamline on the wrong side of one of the HSTs from each pair.

6. Place each pair right sides together, Nest the seams with the light matched to the dark. Sew ¼" away from both sides of the drawn line on each pair. Cut on the drawn line. Press.

7. Trim each Hourglass to 3" × 3". Make 432.

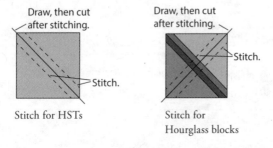

Draw, then cut after stitching.   Stitch.

Stitch for HSTs

Draw, then cut after stitching.   Stitch.

Stitch for Hourglass blocks

ASSEMBLE AND FINISH THE QUILT

1. Sew together 18 blocks to make each row. Rotate every other block 90° clockwise. Press.

2. Sew together the 24 rows. Press.

3. Layer the pieced top with batting and backing. Quilt and bind as desired.

Rotate every other block in a row.

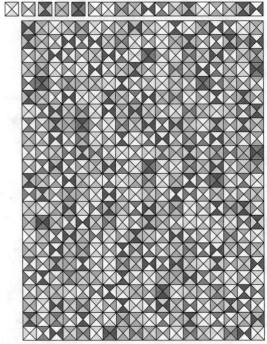

Quilt assembly

*Turn the page for a preview ------------------------------➔
of the next book in A Quilting Cozy series.*

PROJECT

2nd edition includes instructions to make the featured quilt

Sea Bound

a quilting cozy

Carol Dean Jones

Preview of *Sea Bound*

Barney's tail wagged his whole body as he tried to keep all four feet on the floor and not jump up on his favorite person. "Good dog, Barney! I missed you, too," Sarah replied as she stooped down to hug her special friend.

The light on the answering machine was blinking. Sarah hung up her sweater as she listened to the message. "Hi, Sarah. This is Vicky Barnett. We have a patient who I think could really benefit from your visits. Please give me a call."

Sarah played the message twice, wondering what Vicky had in mind. Vicky was the volunteer coordinator at the local nursing home. When Sarah first moved to Cunningham Village, she had hoped to get a volunteer assignment in the nursing home, but her initial tour of the facility had caused her to rethink her plan. She was having enough trouble adjusting to life in a retirement village, and she was afraid that spending time there would make the adjustment that much harder.

Sarah thought about that first visit to the nursing home and the environment of despair she found on the upper floors. *But that was over two years ago*, she reminded herself. Now she had friends, activities, a wonderful dog, and even a gentleman friend. She giggled at the thought. *Nearly seventy years old and I have a boyfriend!*

In fact, Sarah met Charles through Vicky and the volunteer program. Sarah had been reluctant to work in the facility back then. Even so, Vicky had thought Sarah could be helpful to a particular gentleman who had recovered from a massive stroke and was now living independently in the Village. He had been isolating himself, and he needed help getting connected to the community. Upon meeting, they both realized they had met before. Charles had been the police officer sent to her home twenty years earlier to inform her of her husband's death. Over the past two years, Sarah and Charles had developed a deep friendship from her point of view and a deep love from his.

"Well, that referral of Vicky's sure worked out," Sarah said aloud with a smile. "Perhaps I should give her another chance."

Hearing her voice, Barney assumed she was talking to him. He wagged his tail and looked deep into her eyes, hoping she was talking about treats or perhaps a walk in the park. Sarah laughed at the anticipation and love he was able to express simultaneously. "Okay, fella. Let's go for a walk." Barney ran to the kitchen and clumsily pulled his leash off the hook. He dragged it to Sarah with the buckle bouncing across the floor. Sarah snapped it on, and the two friends eagerly headed out the front door.

"Where are you going with that homely mutt?" Sophie called from her porch across the street.

"He's not homely," Sarah called to her good-naturedly, knowing Sophie didn't mean it but also knowing he had a rather straggly look about him. "Do you want to take a walk with us?" she called to Sophie.

"Surely you jest," Sophie hollered, "but stop in for tea on your way back." Sarah waved her acceptance. Sophie put her book aside and reached for her cane. "… and perhaps a big slice of cake," Sophie added to herself as she moved slowly toward her kitchen. She was having trouble moving. Her back and shoulders were hurting and her side was bruised, but that was well concealed under her shirt. Her friend Andy had asked her just that morning why she was limping so badly. She didn't tell him about her fall in the bathroom the previous day. Just like she hadn't told Sarah the week before when she fell in the parking lot getting out of her car. "It's nobody's concern," Sophie told herself as she lifted the cover off the cake plate and prepared to cut two large pieces. *Nobody's concern.*

By the time Sarah and Barney appeared at Sophie's kitchen door, they were both panting. Sophie had a pan of water ready for Barney and a glass of ice tea ready for Sarah. "Sit," Sophie said to Sarah in her usual abrupt manner, pointing toward the table. Barney sat. Both women laughed, and Sarah pulled a treat out of her pocket.

As the two women enjoyed Sophie's latest culinary creation made with her three favorite ingredients—butter, sugar, and dark chocolate—they caught up on the latest gossip and laughed at Sophie's rendition of who said what to whom at the community meeting the night before. Sophie could imitate anyone and frequently did, often right to the person's face!

PREVIEW

"I got a call from Vicky today," Sarah began, anticipating Sophie's objections. Sophie's husband had died in the nursing home following several years of progressive deterioration.

"And …?" Sophie responded with a frown.

"She said she has a patient she would like me to visit."

"And …?"

"I know how you feel about this, Sophie, but we can't hold what happened to your husband against the people that might need us now."

"You do what you want, but you won't catch me near that place. They murdered my husband."

"Sophie, you know that isn't true." But Sarah knew there was no arguing with her. Sophie had spent many months sitting with her husband, remembering their love and their years together, while he sat wondering who it was that sat with him. She had brought in specialists trying to reach him, but he continued to disappear into the abyss of Alzheimer's. No one could stop it, but Sophie, to this day, blamed the nursing home.

Changing the subject, Sarah asked, "Didn't I see Andy and Caitlyn coming out of your house this morning?" Andy lived in the next block and was younger than Sarah and Sophie by about ten years. Andy was a gentle man with a troubled past. Earlier in the year, his fourteen-year-old daughter, Caitlyn, came to live with him. Andy and Caitlyn, who had previously been strangers, had become inseparable.

"Yes," Sophie responded. "They stopped by to see if I wanted to go out with them today. They were off to the mall to get Caitlyn's school clothes, and I guess Andy feels insecure about it."

"I think that girl can choose her own wardrobe without much help from her father. That's one independent young lady!" Sarah said with a proud smile. She thought of Caitlyn as family. Andy and Caitlyn had no relatives, and Caitlyn had immediately gravitated toward Sarah as a surrogate grandmother.

Cunningham Village was a retirement community in Middletown, a small Midwestern town. The Village had separate houses and one-story villas connected in groups of five for the independent residents. Sarah and Sophie lived across the street from one another in the villas. There were several apartment buildings with elevators and assistance for those residents who needed help with their care, and there was a nursing home for those needing total care. Sophie, who enjoyed the occasional gallows humor, would announce, "Cunningham Village offers the whole package, from active retirement living to a cemetery just a stone's throw away!"

As Sarah and Barney were saying goodbye to Sophie, a car pulled up across the street in Sarah's driveway. An unfamiliar man got out and hurried to her door. "I'd better get over there," Sarah announced. "Whoever that is seems to be in a hurry."

"Sarah Miller?" the stranger asked hesitantly as Sarah approached.

"Yes," she responded with a puzzled look. She thought she would recognize him once she got closer, but although he looked slightly familiar, she couldn't place him. She glanced back at Sophie's house and saw that Sophie was waiting at the door, protectively watching over her.

"Hi," the man said. "I'm Gary Pearson, Rose's grandson."

"Oh my! Gary! I'm so embarrassed. I didn't recognize you. What are you doing in Middletown?"

"It's no wonder you didn't recognize me," Gary responded, beaming. "It's been over twenty years since we saw each other!" They exchanged an awkward hug, and Sarah waved to Sophie that all was well. "My company needed someone to go to Hamilton to meet with some buyers. Since Hamilton is only a forty-five-minute drive from Middletown, I volunteered to make the trip so I could come see you."

"Well how sweet of you, Gary!" In a more serious tone, Sarah laid her hand on the man's arm and said, "I'm sorry about your grandmother. Aunt Rose was very special to me. I wanted to come to the funeral, but …"

"No explanation necessary, Sarah. No one expected you to make that trip. Portland is a long trip to make for just a day or two."

Gary put his arm around Sarah's shoulder, and they walked into her house. Barney ran up to meet them, but seeing Gary, he backed away and looked at Sarah. "It's okay, fella. He's one of the good guys."

Gary chuckled, and Sarah noticed how his eyes twinkled when he laughed. Sarah hadn't seen her Aunt Rose for many years, but in that moment she could see her eyes. She gave his arm a tender squeeze and asked if he would like a cup of coffee.

"I could use a whole pot of coffee, if you don't mind." He chuckled and followed her into the kitchen. "I took the red-eye and didn't get much sleep. I have a room in Hamilton, but I drove directly to Middletown as soon as I checked in so we could have a few hours together. I'll be tied up in meetings the rest of the week."

PREVIEW

"How about a little food with that coffee?" she asked.

"If it's not too much trouble, that would be great."

Knowing he had been flying all night, she decided breakfast was in order. While he sat at the table talking about his job, Sarah fried bacon and eggs and put on a fresh pot of coffee. Barney kept his distance until they were both settled down at the kitchen table. He then cautiously checked out this new person. Before Sarah brought Barney home from the shelter, he had experienced a life on the street that Sarah didn't know much about, but she certainly noticed that he was cautious around some people.

The two cousins sat in the kitchen for a couple hours, talking about past experiences and catching each other up on happenings in their respective families. Sarah saw Gary's eyelids growing heavy. "How about a nap?" she offered.

"I'm embarrassed to say that's just what I need about now. Would you mind?"

"Not at all," Sarah responded cheerfully. "You take a nap, and when you wake up we'll plan our afternoon." Sarah led him to the guest room. She had converted it into a sewing room the previous year but had a comfortable futon for visitors. She removed a quilt and a pillow from the oak cabinet and placed them on the futon.

"What a beautiful quilt," Gary remarked. "Grandma had said you were quilting now. Did you make this one?"

"I sure did. You lie down and take a nap. When you wake up, I'll show you the few quilts I've made, and we'll decide what to do with the rest of our day."

"I have something to talk to you about, too, but we'll save that for later," Gary said, loosening his tie.

Once Gary was settled down in the guest room, Sarah hurried to the phone to return the call to Vicky.

"Hello, Vicky. It's Sarah Miller returning your call. I'm at home now if you want to call me back." *Answering machines!* Sarah knew they were necessary and often helpful, but she still yearned for the days when you called a person and you either reached them or you didn't. *So simple,* she thought.

Sarah tidied up the kitchen and took a roast out of the freezer for dinner, assuming Gary would want to stay. If he did, she thought she would invite Charles, too. She decided she would invite Charles either way. She put in a quick call to him and left him a message. *Sometimes answering machines are very helpful,* she thought with a smile.

After that was done, Sarah felt a bit at loose ends. She had planned to work on the quilt she was making, but Gary was in the sewing room. She needed to run by the fabric shop for some thread and another yard of her background fabric, but Gary was parked in the driveway and she couldn't get her car out. She was momentarily baffled, but looking down into Barney's eyes, she realized what she could do.

Sarah wrote a quick note in case Gary woke up, telling him she was out for an hour or so. She latched Barney's leash onto his collar, and again the two hurried out the door and up the street toward the nursing home. Once they reached the main entrance, however, they hesitated. Sarah wasn't sure Barney was welcome inside. She tied him to a post and stepped in to ask. She came back out a few minutes later, smiling, and told Barney happily, "You're in!"

They headed up the hall to the volunteer office. Sarah stuck her head in, holding Barney back in the hallway. "Is Vicky in?" she asked the receptionist.

"I hear a familiar voice!" Vicky came out of her office to greet Sarah. Vicky looked pleased to see Sarah and Barney. "We could use Barney here, too," Vicky said. "Have you considered getting him trained as a visitor?"

Sarah admitted she had never thought of it, but it sounded like something the two of them would enjoy. She said she would look into it.

Barney curled up at Sarah's feet as the women talked about the current assignment.

PREVIEW